I Am Her
She Is Me

Birdie Thorn

DEDICATION

This is for my best friend who is the light at the end of the maze. To my husband who encouraged me to keep going even when I didn't want to. To my dad, who gives the best free advice.

"Be patient and learn that balance."

TRIGGER WARNINGS

This book contains references to suicide ideation and some sexual content.

ACKNOWLEDGMENTS

Thank you so much to Fluky Fiction LLC for bringing my
book to life!

THE BEGINNING
CHAPTER 1

Eyes closed, I can feel the heat of the sun filtering through my bedroom window, signaling me to wake up. Start the day. But I won't; I ignore the warm touch and keep my eyes closed. I want to be alone with myself, free from all inner noise. At least momentarily. The noise will come. It always does. Thoughts that trigger more unhealthy thoughts, followed by obsessive actions. The internal manifesting itself into the physical. A cyclical schism. Even something as mundane as cleaning my perpetually messy apartment can set me totally off course. From that point, it's a psychological rollercoaster of frantically over analyzing everything I have/haven't done, need to do, or shouldn't do at all.

Over time, I've made multiple lists to help me stay on track. Where are they? Well…they're lost. Not on purpose, but it is what it is. Sometimes, I wonder, *Maybe…if I clean my apartment…I could find the lists again. Maybe just one…*

You'd think my apartment wouldn't be too hard to clean since it's only 500 square feet, but you're wrong. No matter what, I always lose those lists. Every. Damn. Time. Just *poof*—gone. You couldn't imagine all the things I've started, then promptly abandoned for something else. Forever unfinished, but not forgotten. One thing I know for sure: tonight's my thirty first birthday. Time to hit up the ATM for some funds.

My main financial pipeline comes courtesy of my dad. He died two years ago, leaving me a significant chunk of money in his absence. To this day, I don't understand the how or why of it. I mean, I refused to speak to the guy for over eight years. Nearly a decade of monk-like silence between us. Maybe I got the money because I'm the only family he has left—one of the few benefits of being an only child. Nonetheless, I am grateful; holding down a job for longer than six months is nearly impossible for me.

The longest stint I've had at any job was about a year. I always start out great, no problems at all. Everything's perfectly fine. Then, at some point, my mind betrays me. Bipolar isn't something you can just jot down on your resume, like a diploma or phony reference. Understand this: my struggle has never been *getting* a job, it's *keeping* it. When I'm manic, I become overly confident. And what employers doesn't love a confident employee, right? Confidence = competence. Given that, would they still hire me if they knew that version of me was manic? Probably not. Don't get me wrong; Manic Me is great and all, but she can't stick around for too long. She's like the highest of highs. She takes me to top of the world.

Honestly, the last job I had was actually one of my favorites. I was working as the Executive Assistant to the Vice President of a big construction company. My job was to understand a little bit about everyone's duties, especially the V.P.'s. In a short amount of time, I became very successful. Moreso, I was liked. I was the version of me that I'd always wanted to be. Definitely one of the more desirable effects of mania is the delusion of invincibility. That feeling of being able to take on the whole world. Ironically, it was this same false bravado that made me so damn good at my job.

But, like clockwork, depression found its way back in again. Despite all preemptive measures, depression always ends up crashing the party.

I helped the Vice President create a new system to lower costs and improve profit. Everything was working out just as it should. No hiccups or obvious fault lines. We were making more money than ever. I hoped this would result in a raise for those who deserved it most—the hard-working people out in the field. Instead, a good chunk of them got an email announcing they were being laid off. "Thanks for your hard work...now, don't let the door hit you on your way out." The extra money we made from utilizing the new system was allocated to those at the top. That's when I finally experienced the defeat. The crash.

Mania and depression do have one thing in common: they often drive me to do things that I wouldn't normally do. I find myself trying to salvage unsalvageable things—i.e. old friendships, family, and past relationships. If I do manage to successfully salvage something during mania, the inevitable crash that follows ruins it. Then, it ruins me.

Most people hear the term *bipolar* and immediately think of an unhinged person—stained straightjackets, plastic lunch trays, and padded white walls. They imagine someone who is mentally broken, doing unhinged, dangerous things. They see someone who, instead of being a productive member of society, chooses to squirrel themselves away in a dark room for weeks on end. Although there might be some truth to these stereotypes, it doesn't come close to showing the whole picture. I've spent many years trying to understand my own bipolar. In the long process of self-realization, I've managed to recognize that there are five main phases that I cycle through. Dangerous, wild things might happen in one phase, while hiding away in a dark room consumes another. I will say, no matter what the phase, there's going to be a heaping teaspoon of "unpredictability" mixed in.

100% guaranteed.

Everyone's personal experiences differ—that's a given. For me, I spend most of my time trying to maintain a neutral state. A real sense of contentment, I guess. Whatever you want to call it, I'm rarely successful. I feel like I exist between two polar states: super happy and unbearably sad. Unfortunately, I'm stuck in my lows more often than my highs. When I go low, I stay low for long periods of time. I have other moods that are less extreme, but they don't do damage like mania and depression do. Not even close.

This is the best way I can describe one of my depressive episodes:

Think of my brain as a big maze. You enter, alone. It's pitch black in every direction you turn. Using your limited senses, you must find your way to the light at the end before the maze consumes you. The maze, it doesn't want you to escape. Not only is it impenetrably dark, but loud. The loudness comes from the sounds that emotions make. An army of banging drums represents the sound of anger. A massive group of people, all squawking at once, is the sound of chaos. The shrill screeching of unseen women is fear. Thunder and lightning, the sound of distraction. And, last but not least, barking dogs for anxiety.

On your journey through the maze, you will encounter false doors that lead to nowhere. Immeasurable misnomers and dead ends. There will be plenty of puzzles to solve, but not enough pieces to do it. There will be pointless riddles and hard questions, all without answers. Worst of all, there will be pain. So, so much pain! And when you finally do reach the end of the maze, and you see that first faint flicker of light, you won't believe your eyes. After all you've been through, you won't trust your own senses anymore. The maze is designed to deceive. To dismantle. You will start to ask yourself: *How do I know I've truly found my way to the other side?*

Lucky for me, my best friend, Kate, is always there to help pull me back out. She assures me that what I'm seeing is real. Or not real.

I try my best to catch triggers before they set major mood swings into motion. Sometimes, I can do it. Other times, I miss. This—right now—is one of those misses. Currently, I am sliding into mania. Already, I know this one will be hard to hide from Kate. I hate to admit this…but I enjoy the euphoria that mania can induce. There isn't a single drug out there that can properly replicate it. Normally, I do everything possible to prevent mania, but this time is different. I haven't been this happy in a long, long time. Besides…what could just a little taste hurt?

When I hear the deadbolt on the apartment door slide open, I decide it's time to finally open my eyes. Only one other person has the key to my apartment, and that's Kate. I hear her singing "Happy Birthday" as she comes through the front door. She continues to sing as she comes down the hall, her voice drawing nearer. As Kate peers around the corner, I look over at her just as she finishes singing. Laughing, she bounds across the room and bellyflops onto my bed, landing right next to me. I pull the covers up over my head and groan.

"It's March fourth! Get up, birthday girl!" Kate says excitedly. "Why are you still in bed? You know it's almost two p.m., right? Were you up all night again?" Before I have time to answer, she quickly adds, "We need to keep track of how often you pull these all-nighters. Definitely not good."

I get a small twinge in my chest when Kate says "we" when discussing my bipolar. It literally hurts my heart to know someone loves me enough to willingly take on my illness with me so I don't have to suffer alone. Kate would never let me suffer alone, even if I thought I deserved to. Without a doubt, she has been the single most consistent person in my life for the past ten years. I don't know what I'd do without her.

We first met on my twenty-first birthday. I had decided to go out to the club by myself since I didn't have any close friends. I didn't know it then, but I was full blown manic at the time. My birthday tends to do that for me—trigger mania. It's funny; being manic when I met Kate was probably a good thing. The mania gave me the confidence to talk to her. We were both in the bathroom at a dance club. Kate was standing in one corner with some friends, fiddling with a loose bra strap.

I don't know why, but I approached her and asked, "What's wrong?"

"My bra strap broke." I could tell she was seriously

bummed out.

"What's your size?"

Cautiously, she replied, "Thirty-four C."

"Well, friend, today is your lucky day." I reached behind my back, under my shirt, and unhooked my bra. Slipping the straps down off over my shoulders, I stealthily pulled the bra out through the front of my shirt.

As if just witnessing a magic trick, Kate gawked at me, unsure of what to say. She stared at me as if I was certifiably insane. Little did she know how close to the truth she really was.

Finally, Kate flung her head back and laughed. "Seriously?"

"Rarely, but tonight…yes," I responded, handing the bra forward. Kate then asked for my number so that she could return the bra to me the next day. I agreed and gave her my number.

I watched as Kate smiled and walked out of the bathroom with her friends.

The next day, I got a text that read:

Hey, this is Kate. The girl who took your bra.

So, naturally, I responded, *Enjoy her, Kate. She is loyal and won't quit on you. I promise.*

Prior to that day, I thought everyone was exactly like me. No better, no worse. I didn't realize that what I was experiencing wasn't normal. I didn't know that I was about to take a nosedive directly into the dark abyss of depression either. Not even a week later, I ended up in a psychiatric hospital. When I was released 72 hours later, I checked my phone to see that I had several missed calls and texts from

Kate. I read through them while standing outside the hospital. She was trying to return the bra. The last text read:

I swear, I'm not some weirdo serial killer if that's why you aren't responding. If you would rather meet in a public space to get your bra, I'm okay with that. Whatever works for you.

Without much thought, I responded back, *Okay. Would you consider a mental hospital to be a weird place to meet up?*

Kate came, picked me up, and brought me home. No questions asked why I was even in the hospital. We've been friends ever since, and the rest, as they say, is history.

Rolling onto my side, I keep the blanket over my head as I face Kate. Then, as slow as possible, I pull the blanket down until just my eyes are visible. Our stares meet. With her face drifting only a few inches from mine, she starts to giggle.

"Happy birthday, my beautiful friend," Kate whispers. "I think thirty-one looks amazing on you already."

"You are too good to me, Kate. Really."

Kate immediately stands up on the bed and plants one foot on each side of me locking me in on either side. With no way out, I'm forced to roll over onto my back and look up at her. She is perfect, rooted with long legs that seem to go on for days. Standing at roughly 5'9", she has amazing blonde hair and sparkling blue eyes. These features are framed by the most beautiful pale white skin you could imagine. Flawless. Like faraway stars, a constellation of freckles pepper the finer features of her face. Kate's a sweet spitfire, bursting with light and energy. She is strong, smart and—most of all— humble.

"So, here's the plan!" Kate says while bending over toward me. "We're going to get up, get dressed, go to dinner, and then go out to dance. Sam, Mags, and Sylvia are meeting us at your favorite dance spot…The Warehouse!"

True: The Warehouse *is* my favorite spot. It's one of those dance clubs where they hand out neon body paint as you walk in. The entire club is lit only by blacklights. For those who might not know, the body paint looks amazing under blacklights! Otherworldly. Also, they play music so loud that it's impossible to think straight. I especially like that part. Sometimes, my thoughts get so loud that I can't concentrate. When I listen to loud music, it drowns out the chatter in my head.

"Can we skip dinner, please?" I ask as I avert my gaze to the side. I regret the words as soon as they leave my lips. Kate, still on the bed, raises one judgmental eyebrow and plops down on top of me.

"Ugh, Kate, your big butt! I can't breathe!" I grunt.

Refusing to move, she barks back, "We are *not* skipping out on dinner! Don't even try that shit with me. Not today." Now nose to nose with me, Kate sternly adds, "Sarah Cole Reeves…we cannot do birthday shots on an empty stomach. Not eating plus partying all night equals disaster. C'mon, you should be puking at the end of the night, not the beginning." Kissing my forehead, Kate rolls off the bed and heads straight to my closet.

As she begins rummaging through my closet, Kate turns back to ask, "Can I help you pick out an outfit for tonight?"

"Sure. Whatever…"

I instantly regret asking to skip dinner. Another unwelcome side effect of mania is a total loss of appetite. Even if I'm feeling physical signs of hunger, I just can't seem to slow myself down long enough to actually eat anything. I just get distracted. My mind and body start to feel like a bee's nest, buzzing with internal energy. Kate knows better than anybody that this is a sign that I'm manic. I don't want her to have to worry about me. I need to convince her that this isn't what she thinks it is.

"You know what?" I start to say in a not-so convincing tone of normalcy. "I'm really craving Mexican food right now. Wow, I'm starving!"

From the open closet, Kate glances back over her shoulder at me. Somehow, I manage a small smile in return. As she turns back to keep rummaging, I get the feeling that she knows everything. The jig is up. There's no way she doesn't know that I'm manic. My poor attempt at deception didn't fool anyone.

Eventually, Kate pulls an outfit from the closet and walks it into the bathroom. When she returns, she stops by the couch with hands planted on her hips, looks around at my disheveled apartment. I know she isn't judging me. Well…not too harshly anyway. To be fair, it is pretty messy.

"How about you jump in the shower while I clean this place up a little?" Kate asks from the other end of the room. Before I even have time to respond, she's started folding some of the wrinkled clothes scattered across my couch. "But hurry up. I want to head out soon!"

I look around my apartment. The main layout is L-shaped in design. Big end, turn, little end. Pretty simple. There's a long hallway right when you enter. On the right-hand side of the hall is a door that leads to the bathroom. On the left-hand side, a doorway to my tiny kitchen. Continuing down the main hall, past the kitchen and bathroom, is an opening into the living room area. My tiny closet sits on the right side of that, next to the couch. Turning left at the very end of the hall, you'll encounter a perfectly square room. My bed occupies one whole side of the room, a table flanking each side of the bed. There are two windows in total. I can see out of one perfectly from my bed. The other window is at the other end of the room where the couch is. There is a short coffee table in front of the couch. Small but quaint.

Reluctantly, I climb out of bed and head for the bathroom. As I walk past Kate, I purposely tip over the pile of towels she has folded. As I laugh, she quickly spins around and pinches the back of my arm. Still laughing, I continue towards the bathroom. When I get there, I see the outfit Kate picked out for me hanging on the back of the door. Judging by her choices, it's obvious that she's planning on having one hell of a night. I can't wait; a night out with Kate is *always* a good night.

I hurry up, take a shower, and finish getting ready. As I walk back out into the living area, I'm shocked by how clean my apartment is. It's truly impressive how much she got done in such a short period of time. Kate, sitting on the bed with her legs crossed, had already changed her outfit—a black bodycon dress and matching heels.

"Took you long enough!" she says as she scoots off the bed. I look over at the clock next to the bed. 4:30 p.m. I'm shocked by the realization that I was in the bathroom for nearly two hours. Long lapses of unaccountable time—yet another sign that Kate will pick up on, I'm sure.

Putting all that stuff off to the side, I look Kate dead in

the eye and say, "Let's go then!"

From there, we head outside to catch a cab. Off to the restaurant we go.

CODEPENDENCY
CHAPTER 2

Walking into the crowded restaurant gives me a boost of happiness. As Kate walks up to the hostess stand to check us in, I take a moment to look around at all the people. Among the crowd, there's a man and woman, maybe in their mid-twenties, smiling and talking to each other. I notice that the man is staring at the woman with such love in his eyes. As if, in that very moment, she is the only thing in the world that matters to him. I know that look well; I'm addicted to it. So much so that I'll destroy who ever dares give it to me. Why? Because symptoms of my bipolar. I've always been the kind of person to hide my issues until I can't any longer. Paranoia, insecurities, guilt, and impulsiveness are my invisible shackles.

Suddenly, I hear someone screech from behind me, "Sarah, you sexy bitch!"

Right away, I know this voice. It's my casual friend, Mags.

Smiling, I turn around and evenly respond, "True enough…I am a sexy bitch."

I watch Mags, Sylvia, and Sam all gather around me. I consider all of them to be casual friends, but, in truth, Kate is my only true friend. Even before Kate, I didn't really have any friends. This was by choice. Sam, Sylvia, and Mags all went to nursing school with Kate. We first met about five years ago when Kate invited us out. We all got along okay. If it wasn't for Kate, though, I doubt this would be the case. Without her involvement, I'm not sure they would even give me the time of day.

They know I have bipolar, but they have no clue of what that entails. Not that I think they would care to know anyway. I purposely keep them all at arm's length, which is closer than most people get. Except for Kate, of course. They don't know how bad my depression gets, or even about my childhood. They don't know how I pay my bills. All they know about me is what's on the surface for all to see.

Mags gives me a big hug. She has a wafting fragrance of peonies, which I personally love. Like me, Mags is short in stature, only 5'3". She has long, curly black hair, blue eyes, and tan skin. Mags is as genuine as she is beautiful. Sam and Sylvia, on the other hand, are boy/girl twins who are also best of friends. They share the same burnt red hair and shimmering blue eyes. Sylvia is 5'9" and Sam is easily 6'2", placing them in supermodel territory.

As an only child, I've always envied their tightknit friendship. My parents had me when they were only eighteen. They were high school sweethearts, until they weren't. Eventually, they despised each other. And, in turn, despised me. When I was fourteen, they finally got divorced. Sadly, their divorce is one of the best childhood memories I have.

For as long as I can remember, my mom struggled with mental health issues while my dad was a full-time drunk. Thankfully, he was a functioning alcoholic, wise enough to acquire life insurance and hold down a good job. His foresight gifted me with plenty of funds, of which I am currently living off of. If I buckle down and live modestly, I won't need to work another day in my life. Assuming I don't live past fifty. Either way—thanks, Dad.

My mom has been in and out of my life. This is my choice, not hers. The only thing she ever gave me was her mental health problems. To her credit, she has tried to maintain our relationship, but I'm not the easiest person to do that with. I also resent her for passing on this problem to me. I know it hurts her that we aren't close.

Soon, Sam and Sylvia both walk up to hug me.

"Happy birthday, Sarah," Sylvia says.

From behind Sylvia, Sam hands me a card and eagerly says, "This is from both of us. You're going to love it."

Since I hate opening cards in front of people, I tuck the envelope into my purse for later. Thankfully, they already know this.

"Thanks, guys, I am so glad you both could make it."

Kate calls over to us; our table is ready.

Once we are seated, we order the first round of drinks. When they arrive, Kate asks everyone to quiet down so she can make a toast. Right away, I feel my face turning red. I hate when all the attention is centered on me, all those prying eyes and ears. Regardless, there's no stopping her now.

"Let's all raise our drinks to my very best friend," Kate warmly says, tears now brimming her bright eyes. "I don't know what I would do without you, Sarah. You make my life better every single day just by being you! CHEERS!"

Everyone clinks their drinks together and takes a drink. As we all take a drink, I notice that Mags and Sylvia are giving each other a certain "look." Without much thought, I deduce that it has something to do with Kate's speech. Ever since Kate dropped out of nursing school, I've felt a shift in their energy whenever they are around me. Kate swears she didn't drop out because of me, but we all know she did. It happened during a mental breakdown I had that lasted eight long months.

It's hard for people to understand why Kate is so committed to me—to our friendship. Hell, it took me a long time to understand myself. As much as Kate and I love each other, we do have a very codependent relationship. Kate is a source of comfort to me, like a baby with a favorite blanket or toy. I guess I remind Kate of her late brother, Trevor. She's made it her main purpose in life to prevent me from ever harming myself like he did.

Kate grew up in an ideal home. Her mom, Pam, and dad, John, both had college degrees in accounting. They opened their own accounting business in a small town just outside of Phoenix, one that has remained prosperous to this day.

After graduating college, getting married, and starting a career together, Kate's parents began trying for a baby. Pam got pregnant with Trevor rather quickly. The pregnancy and delivery were also relatively easy. When Trevor turned three, it was obvious that he would thrive as an older sibling. So, Pam and John tried for another baby. Unlike Trevor, this took many years of trying, but to no avail. They took this as a sign that Trevor was supposed to be an only child and were okay with it.

When Trevor was a little over twelve, Pam got sick. So sick, in fact, that she ended up in the hospital. While she was there, the doctors took a urine sample and ran a pregnancy test. Well, the test came back positive. Turns out, Pam was nearly seven weeks pregnant. Everyone was shocked by this, especially since they had stopped trying years prior. And just like everything in their lives, the couple rolled with the unexpected news.

Kate was born on Trevor's thirteenth birthday. Most kids would've been less than thrilled to have to share their birthday with a younger sibling, but not Trevor. He loved that his baby sister was born on his birthday. In fact, he told anyone willing to listen that Kate was by far his favorite birthday gift. Ever.

This goes without saying, but Kate and Trevor were close. The thirteen-year age gap didn't affect their relationship one bit. They went everywhere together. Trevor never had many friends and Kate benefited from that. She's told me stories about how they used to go to the mall, zoos, and movies together. They were more than just siblings; they were best friends. When Trevor had to go off to college, which was a two-hour drive away, Kate really struggled. His goal was to become a nurse. Kate was proud of Trevor for this, but also sad that her best friend would be moving so far away. Luckily, he came home every weekend to see his little sis. The two just couldn't stand to be apart.

Kate's favorite memory of Trevor was on her eighth birthday, his twenty-first. It was a Friday, the day Trevor usually came back home to visit for the weekend. Not this time. Instead, Trevor called Kate early that morning and told her that he would be staying at school to celebrate with friends. This news crushed Kate; this would be her first birthday without her big bro by her side.

Around midnight on that same night, while Kate was lying in bed, she was awakened by the sound of her bedroom door slowly opening. Scared, she hid her head under the covers. As slow footsteps moved closer to her bed, little Kate began to cry. Right when she was about to yell for her parents, the blankets were yanked off away, leaving her exposed. To Kate's great surprise, she looked up to see Trevor standing at her bedside. Silently, he motioned for her to stay quiet.

"TREVOR! You scared me!!" Kate yelled as she got up on her knees in bed.

"Shhh, be quiet. Don't wake up Mom and Dad," Trevor whispered. Dropping the handful of sheets, he sat down on the outer edge of the bed.

Happy to see her big brother, Kate jumped up and wrapped her arms lovingly around his neck. "Oh, I've missed you so much, Trevor."

"Missed you more, you little shit."

"Hey, don't say bad words," Kate gasped, pulling back from Trevor to plant her hands on her hips. "Aren't you supposed to be at the college right now?"

"Yeah, but that wasn't gonna stop me from missing our special day!"

"I'm eight, Trevor! Isn't that old?!" Kate excitedly shouted, as if she had just remembered that it was their birthday.

"I know, I know. Do me a favor and close your eyes. No peeping."

Giggling, Kate bowed her head and covered her eyes.

Trevor reached behind his back, pulling out two sets of

Mini Mouse themed headbands. He put one set on his own head before crowning Kate with the other. Once both set of fake mouse ears were secured, he leaned forward and whispered, "Okay…open your eyes…"

Kate's jaw dropped as she looked back and forth from Trevor to his fake ears. Before she could say anything, Trevor turned and pointed to a Mini Mouse suitcase that sat by her open bedroom door.

"So, I was planning on going to Disneyland for my twenty-first birthday…but I was kinda hoping my little shit sister would want to come. What do you think?"

In response, Kate screeched and quickly got to her feet. Like a wild animal, she pounced on Trevor, causing them both to fall back onto the bed. Both laughing, Kate hugged her big brother tight and said, "Thank you, thank you, thank you!"

Like most kids, Kate had always wanted to visit Disneyland. Although it was only a five-hour drive from their home, her parents were always too busy to take her. In their defense, they were busy working so they could pay for Trevor's schooling. I'm sure it wasn't cheap.

After Trevor helped Kate pick out her clothes and get dressed, they packed the Mini Mouse suitcase and snuck downstairs. Once at the front door, Kate stopped and looked back toward the stairs.

"Hm…aren't Mom and Dad going to wonder where I am?" she asked.

"I'll leave them a note. Tell 'em we ran away to join the circus."

Kate giggled, "Okay, Trevor, let's go!"

Kate and Trevor slipped outside to the car. After Trevor put the bags in the backseat, he helped Kate get buckled up. Minutes later, they were on the road—off to the create Kate's most cherished childhood memory. The brother and sister drove to Disneyland on a Friday morning and didn't return until late Sunday night. To this day, she still claims it was the best time of her life.

It was dark when they finally pulled into the driveway at home. Kate was amazed when her parents actually came out to greet them, not mad at all for her overnight disappearing act. Much later, Kate found out that they had known about the trip all along. In fact, they secretly paid for the whole thing.

"What happened, Kate?" her mother jokingly asked. "Did you guys get fired from the circus?"

"I thought you'd be sad if I never came home...so...I quit," Kate joked back. While still sitting in the passenger seat, Kate looked over at Trevor, who was all smiles. Coyly, they winked at each other in mutual understanding.

To Trevor, Pam asked, "Why don't you just stay here tonight and drive back to school in the morning?"

Initially, Trevor was very hesitant about staying over. He kept giving excuses as to why he needed to leave that night. Kate remembered being confused by this; Trevor was never in a hurry to go back to school. When he continued to decline the offer, Kate pleaded with him to stay just one more night. She knew he couldn't tell her no. And she was right—Trevor reluctantly agreed to stay.

"Trevor gets to sleep in my room!" Kate yelled as she ran inside the house. "I'll make up the bed!" She was so excited to get one more night with her best friend. Opening her closet doors, she pulled out her favorite sleeping bag decorated in glittery, rainbow-colored unicorns. With utmost care, she laid it out nicely on the bedroom floor.

When Trevor came by to say goodnight, he couldn't help but laugh. "Kate, I appreciate the gesture, but I have to sleep in my old room tonight."

Kate was offended. She stomped her foot down and crossed her arms, angrily telling him, "But I already made you a bed. Please, this the last time I'll be seeing you 'til next weekend."

Trevor smiled. "Okay okay, you win. I got some homework to do in my room first. In the meantime, get to bed. I'll be back in a little bit."

Kate nodded and gave Trevor a big hug. Suddenly, she got a feeling. A bad feeling. Something seemed off. When she went to pull away from the hug, Trevor continued to hold on. Wrapped in his arms, Kate looked up and gasped; Trevor was crying. His eyes shimmered with tears; his normally youthful face now wrinkled and sad. When the hug was over, Trevor simply turned and walked out of the room. As he left, still facing the open doorway, he said, "I love you, Kate."

This struck Kate as odd. Normally, Trevor would call her a little shit or something playfully mean like that. Typical big brother stuff. Unsure how to react, Kate stammered back, "I-I…I love you too…" Then, she climbed back into bed.

Since the past weekend was jam packed with nonstop excitement and junk food, Kate fell asleep without much trouble.

Very early the next morning, she was awoken by a strange sound in her room. A shuffling sound, awkward footsteps. It was Trevor. He seemed unanchored, his every step Kate watched through squinted eyes as he swayed back and forth. She watched as he made his way over to the glittery rainbow-colored unicorn sleeping bag on the floor. His eyes were big and wide, two blank mirrors of absent light. The sight scared Kate so badly that she couldn't speak or move. Clutching her pillow, she just lay there and watched him slither into the sleeping bag and close his owl-like eyes.

Kate, grabbing her Mini Mouse stuffed toy, slowly climbed out of bed and approached Trevor. "Trevor, are you okay?" Trevor incoherently mumbled something in response, but she couldn't make it out. That's when Kate noticed that his skin looked pale. Almost phosphorescent. Assuming he was sick, Kate gently lifted his arm and tucked the stuffed toy underneath it. "Thank you, Trevor, I love you most."

She then kissed him on the forehead and got back into bed.

Looking back on those memories as an adult is understandably hard for Kate. Too many mixed emotions, too much joy and sorrow. She was too young at the time to realize that Trevor was suffering from severe depression. Apparently, he had battled with it for most of his life. Kate idolized her big brother so much that she never saw the signs. In her mind, Trevor was nothing short of a perfect person. The best big brother anyone could ever wish to have. What Kate didn't know was that Trevor wasn't perfect. That same night he snuck into her room after Disneyland, he accidentally overdosed on a concoction of pills.

Kate woke up later that morning to find that her brother had died in her favorite sleeping bag.

I know Kate is scared that I might meet the same fate as Trevor; she feels like his death was partly her fault. Kate feels so much guilt for not recognizing the obvious signs. Even though Kate was only eight when Trevor died, she still feels like she could've saved him. Trevor deserved a second chance.

Kate loves me, I know that. I'm her world, as she is mine. I'm aware that she probably sees Trevor in me. The similarities are definitely there. I think, in a lot of ways, Kate sees me as her second chance to save Trevor. And part of me feels guilty for that. I mean, I did just sit back and watch her drop out of nursing school her junior year over my mental breakdown. Never a word of skepticism. Our codependency runs deep, for sure. But seriously, I wouldn't be alive right now if it wasn't for Kate. And Kate would be thriving if it wasn't for me. Irony at its finest.

After the birthday dinner was over, we head outside and catch a cab to the Warehouse. I hope this will take my mind off things, mostly the fact that everyone around me doesn't really like me that much. Oh well, what can you do?

MAN-I-C
CHAPTER 3

I can already hear the pulsing rhythms of The Warehouse as our cab pulls up curbside. Through my side window, I look up at the big, flashing neon sign:

<u>The Warehouse</u>
A Dance Club

The sign is what initially drew me here. What can I say? I'm a sucker for simple, straightforward advertising. Uncomplicated. Straight to the bone. I mean…it's all in the name, right?

From the front seat of the cab, Kate turns and flashes me a mischievous smile. "You ready?"

I smile back. "Always."

The pulsing music gets louder as we step out of the cab. I immediately feel a wave of calmness come over me. As we weave through random groups of people for the entrance, I feel instant relief. Zen.

After clearing the bouncers, we ascended a long, narrow hallway. Several strings of neon lights hang along the ceiling and baseboards like dead snakes. At the very end of the hallway is a single door. Beyond it is an enormous space with high ceilings, every square inch illuminated by strobe and black lights. I'm not surprised to see that there's already tons of people here, neon paint smeared across their bodies. Aside from the music, dancing, and unadulterated fun, everyone is just living in the moment.

Our group quickly moves to a staircase that leads to the upper level. This is where the private tables and couches are. We eventually stop at a table with a sign on it that reads, "Happy 31st birthday, Sarah!"

Once we are all gathered around the table, Kate holds up her phone and cheers, "Woo! VIP for the birthday girl!"

Mags, Sylvia, and Sam join in, "Happy Birthday! Woot, woot!"

I start to giggle as I throw my arms up, "Here's to thirty-one years, baby!"

Just as we all settle in at our table, a server walks up with a serving tray of shot glasses and little tubes of body paint. She's wearing a black mini skirt, black bra, and black combat boots. As she skillfully sets down the tray. I take a glance at the nametag pinned to her bra: Cora.

"You must be, Sarah!" Cora yells at me as she leans across the table to hand out drinks.

"Yes, that's me!"

"Well Sarah, it's time for a birthday shot!"

I already had a few drinks with dinner, so I'm feeling pretty good already. Feeling invincible, I ignore that little voice of reason that reminds me to slow down. Don't dive headfirst. When I get to this point, I tend to overreach and make poor choices. You know what they say: you can only get so high before crashing back down again. My mania is now in full swing, and I hope it stays that way for at least a couple weeks.

We all grab a shot. But before we can tip them back, Kate holds her glass up to make another speech.

"Happy Birthday to my other half! I love you, Sarah!" We smile at each other from across the table. Hooting and hollering, everybody clinks their glasses together and drinks.

The tequila tastes like dirty water, but it makes me feel so good. I close my eyes and savor everything this moment has to offer. I'm so happy. I don't ever want to lose this feeling. I know, in my heart, that it won't last, but for now, I'll just enjoy it.

"Sarah!" I turn around to see Kate and Mags beckoning me to the dance floor. "Sam and Sylvia are heading downstairs to dance! Mags and I are going to grab some drinks…you good?!"

I motion toward the bathroom as I yell back, "Need to pee! Will you grab me a drink?!"

Kate nods and runs over to the bar as I move for the neon pink restroom sign on the other side of the club.

As I walk to the restroom, I can feel the tequila warming my chest. Fluttering and tingling my blood. A mix of mental euphoria, alcohol, and loud music has me feeling like I'm floating across the room. When I reach the neon pink sign, there's a long line leading to the girl's restroom. The line is single file. Covering the opposite side of the wall are huge mirrors. Normally, I hate looking at myself in the mirror, but this time feels different.

Staring at myself, I feel like it's just me in the club. Me, the music, and the mirrors. Everything and everyone else around me fade away. Subtly, I trace the curves of my hourglass figure. If I wasn't so self-conscious, I would think I had the ideal body. My clothes look like they are painted onto my body, breasts heaving from my red halter top. Like silken thread, my long, curly brown hair sweeps past my bra line. The pale glow of my white skin makes my nude eye shadow pop off my eyelids.

Being human is so odd. Why do so many people define beauty by the superficial? Christ, even I do it. I'm a size twelve, never small enough. I'm never tan enough either. We don't define individual beauty by a person's thoughts, morals, or actions. Why can't I just appreciate my body and all it does for me? It keeps me alive while my brain simultaneously tries to kill it.

As I smile at my reflection, a hear a voice behind me say, "She made me smile, too."

All at once, that smile is gone. I don't even want to turn around.

Don't do it, don't do it, I think. *Don't engage in conversation right now. You know how this will end. Just mind your own business and ignore him.* But my curiosity gets the best of me. Seconds later, I turn around.

The man looking back at me is least 6'4". When I crane my head up to look into his eyes, I'm instantly mesmerized. His eyes are mostly blue. Like paint splatter, the left one is flecked with a small brown spot. His hair, a shade of light brown, is lightly tussled. He is wearing a tight black V-neck t-shirt with jeans. He stands with such confidence. Confident people tend to attract confident people. Too bad he doesn't realize that this version of me only appears for about two months out of the year. Somehow, I've managed to catch his attention with a lie.

"She not only smiles, but she also talks, too," I say in a flirty voice.

He responds with a bashful smile. Ahead, the line quickly shortens for the bathroom. Without saying more, I turn and head into the bathroom. I know this is wrong; he doesn't know the real me. Although there's an obvious moral dilemma, my desire for affection will win. It always does. So, I silence the guilt. Just for one night. I can allow myself just *one* night, can't I?

After I use the bathroom, I quickly head back out into the hall, hoping to see the man. Unfortunately, he's long gone. I try not to let the disappointment I feel show. Probably a good thing he isn't here anyway. Some might say *he's* the one who dodged a bullet. And even if I did want him, I know deep down that I don't really *need* him. Swallowing that hard lump of disappointment, I head back to the table. As I get closer, I can see Kate, Mags, Sylvia, and Sam—plus two other men I don't recognize. They stand with their backs to me, casually conversing with everyone at the table. As soon as Kate sees me coming, she starts emphatically waving at me to hurry up. She's probably ready to get painted and get out on the dance floor. Fuckin' finally.

When I reach the table, the mystery men both turn and look at me. My stomach drops as I once again come eye-to-eye with the beautiful stranger from the bathroom line.

"I saw you talking to this guy before you went into the bathroom, so I invited him over!" Kate yells to me from across the table. "Sarah, this is Josh! Josh, Sarah!"

I smile at Josh, and he smiles back. Suddenly, the other

guy he's with leans over his shoulder and announces, "Hey, my name is Brandon! Josh's best friend!"

"Hey, Brandon. This is my best friend, Kate." As I say this, I use Kate like a human shield, throwing her right into the direct line of fire.

Kate, bopping along to the music, yells, "We already met! He doesn't swing our way!" She laughs as she picks up some body paint from the table.

"It's true!" Brandon emphatically agrees. "But, hey, I'm a great wingman!"

Kate jumps back into the conversation to ask, "But are you good at painting?!"

Brandon nods, more than a little excited to help Kate get painted. Usually, Kate and I would paint each other. Since the very first time we came here, it's been just us. I know she's doing this just so Josh and I can be paint-partners. Honestly, Kate is a great wingwoman that way. Always looking out for my best interests. As I lean over and grab a handful of paint tubes, Josh curiously looks down at me. He's so tall that I literally have to crane my neck to ask, "Can I paint you?!"

"Only if I can paint you!" he yells back.

Using an empty chair from the table, I climb up higher. Now, I'm about Josh's height, maybe an inch taller. I then give him all the paint tubes to hold. One by one, I squeeze random globs of paint onto his arms and neck, my fingers tracing shapes, and squiggles all over. When I run my fingers over his biceps, I notice him slightly flex. This makes me laugh.

"My, those are some nice arms!" I say, trying to sound

casual but flirty.

Josh lightly blushes as I continue drawing on his neck and face. Still standing on the chair, I lean back, hand caressing my chin, and admire my work.

"My turn!" Josh says. "Just stay right there!"

I watch as Josh squeezes a whole tube of paint into his palm. As if applying war paint to a fellow warrior, he carefully dips two fingers into the paint and reaches out to me. Josh applies the paint to the shallow dip of my neck, right below my left ear. His fingers then slowly drag downward to my collar bone. He stops and glances up at me before grabbing more paint and squeezing a small amount directly onto my shoulder. In a swooping arc, he then drags the paint down one shoulder, across my chest, and up the other side.

I hate how badly I want Josh to keep touching me. Caressing me. He continues drawing a path down my right arm. In this moment, I feel like the room has gone hollow. There's no music, no people. Just an empty space where only Josh and I could exist. Experiencing this same spark of connectivity. Any hope I had of shrugging this guy off is now null and void. I want him more with each passing moment. No longer want but *need*.

Once we are both fully painted, Josh puts the empty tubes back on the table and helps me down. Jokingly, I ask, "What? You don't want to admire your work?"

"My canvas was already perfect," Josh coyly responds. I laugh as he takes my hand and leads me down the stairs to the main dancing area.

Soon, lights and music surround us. In the middle of the

crowd, Josh tries to say something to me, but I can't hear him at all. Everything is way too loud. I mouth to him that I can't hear him, to which he mouths back, "Never mind." That's when we start dancing. Finally, I feel so free. Completely inhibited. No unwanted thoughts poisoning my mind. Eventually, Kate and the rest of our group make their way out to where we're dancing. Dancing among my people, I close my eyes and just enjoy this moment. These moments of absolute clarity don't come often but, when they do, I make sure to take in every second.

JUST FRIENDS
CHAPTER 4

My head throbs as the heat of the sun coming through my window warms my closed eyelids. Groggily, I open my eyes. I don't remember coming home last night, but here I am. Same old apartment. I *do* remember that last night was a particularly good night. I remember the painting, dancing, drinking… and Josh. Oh my god, Josh. This makes me smile. As I start to sit up in bed, I hear Kate loudly fake cough. She's lying in bed next to me, a mischievous smile creasing her face. As she silently nods over to the couch, I raise my head and squint across the room. There's Josh.

"Good morning," he says.

"Ugh…hello," I awkwardly respond, slowly laying my head back down.

"Well, I need an iced coffee and a shower," Kate announces as she flings the blankets off and gets up. I sit up in bed and scoot my back against the headboard. Josh and I watch as Kate starts to gather her things. As she snatches her phone from the table next to the couch, she randomly looks at Josh and asks, "Why don't you have any social media accounts, hm?" When Josh only flashes her a confused look, she adds, "Yeah, I saw your I.D. last night at The Warehouse. Tried to find you online but you're practically a ghost. So, what're you…a serial killer or something?"

Josh laughs, "Haha, nah, it's nothing like that. I just think social media's toxic. I'm not a serial killer, but I do love me some cereal!"

Kate glanced at me with a blank expression before saying, "Sarah, I think you have this handled! I need to go home and take a shower. Call you later, okay?"

I nod while laughing off Josh's attempt at a joke. As she's walking out the front door, Kate turns back and yells, "Nice meeting you, Josh!"

"You too, Kate!"

When we hear the front door latch shut again, Josh and I both look at each other from across the room and smile.

"I can tell she really cares about you," he says.

I look down at my sheets, unsure of how to respond. I know Kate cares about me. Probably more than anyone else in the whole wide world. She also knows that relationships are a slippery slope for me. The emotional ups and downs of any given relationship can be extremely difficult, if not impossible, for me to handle.

Usually, all's well and good at first. I can fake being normal for a little while. But eventually the truth always comes out. When and how am I supposed to break the news that I have bipolar? Do I wait weeks, months, years? What's the precedent for unloading something fragile like that? How do I even begin to say it? Do I wait until dinner, write it out on a tiny piece of paper, and slide it across the table to them like a murky poem? Or do I just blurt it out in casual conversation like, "Oh, my favorite color? Hm...I like red. I also hate pineapple on pizza and...hm, what else? Oh, I have bipolar. Could you pass the salt, please?"

Snapping me back to the moment, Josh suddenly asks, "So, you want to go get some breakfast or coffee? My treat."

"No, thank you. I've got a lot of stuff to do today. Sorry…"

I don't want Josh to want this. Whatever "this" may be. I know it will only end with someone getting hurt. Or both of us. I watch as Josh stands up and grabs his jacket from the back of the couch. He then walks over to the little desk that sits under my bedroom window, grabs a highlighter, and scribbles something down on a scrap of paper. As he turns and starts to walk toward the bed, I can feel my heart start to race.

Gah, he's so beautiful, I think. *I'm sure I'll be kicking myself later for passing this one up.*

Handing me the paper, Josh smiles and says, "If you change your mind, give me a call." As I reach out to receive the folded paper, Josh swiftly leans down and kisses me on the head. Struck silent, I can only mutely watch as he then turns around and heads for the front door. Once I hear the front door close shut again, I divert my attention to the paper in my hand. It was an old receipt, one I had probably dumped out of my pockets and forgot to throw away. There are only two items listed on the receipt: a Coke and a family-sized bag of Cheetos. Pretty embarrassing, I know. Not exactly making a great first impression. I flip the receipt over to see Josh had scribbled his phone number on the back. God, even his handwriting is beautiful. So neat and fluent. I'm not sure why I'm getting so excited over this; I know there's no way in Hell I can let myself call him. I shouldn't even entertain the idea.

And yet…

Leaning across the messy bed for the end table, I tuck the receipt away in my purse. As I do, I come across the card that Sam and Sylvia gave me last night at dinner. I hate opening things in front of people, so I always wait until I'm alone. Besides, I know the only reason they came out to my birthday party was because Kate probably insisted. With this in mind, I remove the envelope from my purse and sit back in bed. The front of the envelope reads: *Happy Birthday, Sarah!* I open it and pull the card out. As I do, a small piece of paper falls from the card and lands on the bed. Before I divert my attention to the paper, I decide to read the inside of the card first.

Sarah,

We know how much you love excitement and adventure, so we figured this would be the perfect gift for you. Be sure to have lots of fun and take lots of pictures! Happy birthday!

-Sam and Sylvia

Dropping the card, I reach down and flip over the piece of paper. It's a ticket. At the top in bold letters it says,

SEDONA GUIDED TOURS

Admission: 2 people

Right away, I know the only reason I got this gift was to make Kate happy. Not me. Knowing this to be fact, I lay back in bed and blankly stare up at the ceiling.

A guided tour, huh? It's weird; I've lived in Arizona since I was fourteen…and yet… I've never been to Sedona. I think it's only about two hours from here too. Kate hates the heat though. There's no way she's going to want to do this tour with me. Not willingly anyway. Hm, maybe Josh would want to go…

I can make it clear to him that I don't want anything other than friendship. I'm fine with that if he is too. I think I can handle a little friendship with a sexy, tall, funny man. Is that so hard?

Moving a little faster, I lunge back across the bed and reach into my purse for the receipt. I'm just going to send him a text. That's it. Short and simple. Besides, he probably has plans already and will say no.

Quickly, I write out a text:

Hey, Josh, this is Sarah. Would you be interested in going on a guided tour with me in Sedona next week?

After I hit send, I just stare at my phone, waiting intently for a response.

Wow, I'm so awkward. I have no idea what I'm doing right now. I mean, I usually just get in a one-night stand and then ghost them entirely. I never attempt to establish a real connection. Well, until now…

I realize how weird I'm being and decide to put the phone away and take a much-needed shower. Once in the bathroom, already partially undressed, I hear my phone loudly *DING!* from the next room. I burst out of the bathroom wearing only one sock and my bra—no underwear.

Hell yeah! I'd love to go to Sedona with you!

Unable to stop myself from smiling like a drunken idiot, I set my phone down on the nightstand next to the bed and dance my way back to the bathroom. This dancing shuffle stops when I catch a quick glimpse of myself in the bathroom mirror. I'm mortified to see that I have smudged mascara and neon paint smeared all over my face. Leaning over the sink, I look even closer and notice a dried drool line trailing from the right corner of my mouth. I'm mortified that Kate didn't tell me before she left this morning!

Furious, I march back out of the bathroom and grab my phone.

"Hello?" Kate answers, none the wiser.

"Asshole!" I immediately hiss back.

Without much hesitation, Kate starts laughing.

"Why didn't you tell me I looked like total shit!?"

Still laughing, she says, "I assumed you wanted Josh to see the authentic you. The *real* Sarah. Also, that was payback for not telling me I had pepper in my teeth last night. You saw I was trying to flirt with that cute waiter at the restaurant."

Now I'm the one who's laughing. "Oh my God, I didn't see that until after you'd already started talking to him! I swear!"

"Yeah yeah," Kate dismissively responds. "Whatever. So, we are even now?"

"Yeah, we're even."

"Sooo…how's your lover boy—Josh? You guys set a wedding date yet or what?"

"Shut up! He already left. And if you want to gossip about him so bad then just come back over."

In seconds, Kate goes completely silent. Somehow, she

knows that I'm breaking my own rules. "If you insist, lady. I'm on my way."

"Love you, Kate," I say, as if the words will smooth over her growing concerns.

"Love you too, Sarah."

I end the call and head back to the bathroom for the third and final time. Stripping off the last of my clothing, I decide that I'd rather take a bath than a shower. Only when the water is as hot as I can tolerate do I turn off the bathroom light. Entombed in total darkness, I carefully get into the tub, wincing at the searing heat as I lower myself in. Once adjusted to the temperature, I slowly slide my butt down until my body is fully submerged. From there, I lower my head back until only my mouth, nose, and eyes are above water.

Then, there is only silence.

The silence is so thick; nothing from the outside can slip through. This allows me to focus on the noise clouding my brain. Like ugly rubber balls ricocheting back and forth inside a sealed room, these thoughts refuse to go away. They're being recycled—tumble dried inside my head, over and over again. I take a deep breath and try my best to concentrate on just one thing at a time.

What'll my future look like? Will I ever have kids? Get married? Or will I die alone…

Soon, a self-actualized image starts to play out in the foreground of my mind. An ethereal movie of what could/should be.

In it, I'm sitting at a kitchen table. Directly across from me is a little girl. Before her, fanned out across the table, are several pieces of paper. Innocently, the little girl looks to me and asks, "Can you help me with my homework, Mommy?"

Without thought, I rise from my chair and join her on the other side of the table. I was never a commendable student, so, naturally, I struggle to understand what's on the paper. Regardless, I'm determined to help out in any way I can.

Moments later, a man appears from around a nearby corner and asks, "Hey, have you seen my work phone? I can't find it anywhere." Car keys jangling in one hand, paper stuffed folder in the other, I can tell the man is practically frantic. I'm not totally sure why, but he needs my help as well.

Suddenly, from the next room, the dog starts barking.

Crossing the kitchen, I enter the living room and see the dog. He is looking out a bare window—jaws snapping and lips foaming at whatever stood on the other side. Cautiously, I glance out the same window to see a garbage truck lumbering by. It's in this moment that I realize: I forgot to take out the trash.

"Help me, Mommy! I need help!" the little girl starts to holler from her seat at the kitchen table.

I look back to the kitchens open doorway just in time to see the man enter. Still frantic, I watch as he starts crazily opening drawers and flipping over couch cushions. All the while, the dog continues to angrily yip and bark. And there I am, standing smack-dab in the middle of all this chaos. I can't take it. I need to make it stop, so I shove my fingers so far into my ears that I can feel them start to bleed. But the noise only gets louder. Until…

"…Sarah?"

My eyes flutter open at the sound of my name. Sleepily, I look across the now lit bathroom to see Kate. Unsurprisingly, she holds an iced coffee in each hand.

"I didn't even hear you come in," I groan while lazily sliding myself up into a sitting position.

"Deep in thought, aye?" Kate says as she turns to set the coffees down on the nearby countertop. "What were you thinkin' about?"

Shivering knees pulled up to my chest, I bow my head and ask, "Kate…do you think I'll ever live a normal life? Like…with a husband and kids and shit like that?"

"That depends; what's your definition of *normal?*"

"I don't know…being genuinely happy, I guess? Having a real purpose. Something worth living for."

Kate seems to think hard on this for a moment before confidently saying, "I think, ultimately, you can have whatever life you want. The choice is all yours. Always has been. If happiness to you is having a husband and a kid, then I say, go for it."

But is it morally acceptable? I wonder. To get married and have children knowing that I have bipolar. Never mind me; what kind of life would that leave for them? Is it ethical to even pursue such a life knowing that I might pass on these cursed genes? I know if I had a say in it, I'd definitely choose NOT to have bipolar. That's for sure. I don't know…I might need to redefine my own definition of happiness.

I look over at Kate, who's now sitting on the lip of the counter, and say, "So, about last night…" Before I can finish, Kate grabs my coffee and hands it to me.

"Yeah, about last night… What's your plan with Josh exactly?"

I sigh. "Hold on, I should probably be clothed for this conversation. Meet me in the living room in five, okay?"

Smiling, Kate nods, grabs her coffee, and leaves the bathroom.

As I step out of the now cold bath water, I quickly wrap my shivering body in a warm towel. I know Kate's worried about me, but I just don't know what to say. It's been a long time since I've allowed myself the freedom to explore an intimate relationship. For real this time. I also haven't relapsed into a super deep depression for a while now. So, that's something. Been at least two years. I've been especially careful to acknowledge and avoid any major triggers.

You know…maybe it is time to give this whole relationship thing another try…

About five minutes later, I walk out of the bathroom and make my way over to the couch. There, a giant pile of my clean clothes waits for me. Kate must've just pulled them from the drier and put them there. The mighty pile contained many mismatched outfits. With so many layers, it was impossible to tell at this point. Lazily, I start sitting through the pile and eventually pick out sweats and a tank top. I do this because I have no intention of leaving the house today. Kate is sitting on the bed now, quietly scrolling through her phone. Slipping out of the now wet towel, I quickly get dressed, wrap up my still wet hair, then push some clothes over to the side of the couch so I can sit down.

"Okay," I sigh, "let's talk." Attentively, Kate sets her phone down and scoots all the way over to the far edge of the bed so we can be closer. Once I see she's ready to talk, I roll my eyes and ask, "Let's hear it already. What're your concerns?"

For a long moment, Kate remains surprisingly silent. I know this won't last long though; she's accumulating all the right words. Finally, Kate looks up at me and says, "Honestly…I'm worried about you, Sarah. I know I haven't said anything about it until now, but I noticed a couple weeks ago that you were exhibiting signs of mania. At the time, I decided it was probably best to leave it alone, but now I'm not so sure that was the right thing to do. We need to come up with a game plan here. Remember, dating is still fairly new territory for you."

True enough. Dating *is* new territory for me. I've never really been in a serious relationship before. Sure, I've dated and all that fun stuff, but it was always very casual. Fly by night. But I've never felt this way about any man. Makes me wonder: am I just hyper-fixating on Josh because I'm manic or are these feelings legitimate? Sadly, there's no real way for me to be 100% sure.

Kate, never one for beating around the bush, clears her throat to blatantly ask, "Sarah, is this what you *really* want?"

"I mean…yeah, I do, Kate. I really do."

Kate drops her head, allowing her stern gaze to drift downward for a moment. When she looks back up at me, she smiles and says, "Then…we'll figure this out together. You and   me.   Us."

CONFESSION
CHAPTER 5

The last week has gone by unbearably slow. Just a brutal, second by second, stretch. Almost like a self-imposed prison sentence. But I made it through, and today is the day Josh and I go to Sedona together. He plans on picking me up in about fifteen minutes. From there, it's a two-hour long car ride. Just the two of us. Thankfully, Kate helped me pick out my outfit last night. We settled on a white tank body suit with jeans and a pair of black Converse. All suited up and ready for action, I take a moment to look at myself in the full-length mirror that hangs on the bathroom door.

My hair is set high in a messy bun. Pulling the tie out, I watch as each strand falls back down to rest on my shoulders. I judge myself some more and decide I don't like the look. So, I hurriedly yank my hair back up into a bun. I rarely wear my hair down for the simple fact that I'm usually too lazy to style it. I do a couple poses in the mirror to decide which angle looks best. None of them do. As I pretend to Hulk out—flexing my muscles and growling at my own reflection like a rabid grizzly bear—I hear a knock at the front door.

Fuck! Don't panic. Don't panic. Shit...I'm panicking...

Taking a long, deep breath, I quickly leave the bathroom for the front door. When I open it, Josh is standing there just as handsome and statuesque as ever. A living Adonis. Thank God I didn't have beer goggles on the night we first met. I look down and notice that he's holding a brightly decorated gift bag in one hand.

"Hey!" I say with a little too much excitement.

Nervously, he smiles back, trying to match my raw enthusiasm. "Oh, hey!"

We both proceed to stand there in the open doorway and awkwardly stare at each other.

Should I…should I hug him? I ask myself. *No, that might come off as weird. Don't wanna creep him out. Not yet anyway. I guess I could at least invite him inside, right? Is that weird? I guess not…but what if that puts out the wrong idea entirely? Either way, I can't just stand here. Say something!*

Finally, I manage a nervous smile. "Oh…uhm…wanna come in?"

"Yeah, sure."

As Josh moves past me to enter the apartment, I catch the scent of his cologne—a masculine blend of cedar and mango. Wow, not only does he look great, but he smells great too. Slightly intoxicated, I shut the front door and follow Josh down the hallway. As we move forward, I look past him to see the huge pile of clean clothes still stacked on the couch up ahead. The pile now spilled all the way down to the floor, creating a multi-colored avalanche of fabric. Digging in my heels, I pick up my pace to get in front of Josh before he can see the mess. Pivoting quick, I stop him dead in his tracks and say, "Actually, we should probably head out now. Beat the traffic." Arms stretched out, I tried my best to herd him back towards the front door. But it was already too late.

Ever so casually, Josh looks past me, straight to the messy couch. I can feel my face turning red with embarrassment as his eyes shift back down to me.

"Hey, no judgment here," Josh earnestly says. "I mean, who likes doing laundry? Such a time suck. You think that's bad? You should see my laundry pile at home. Mine's on my bed, though."

Nervously, I giggle, "Right. Laundry's the worst."

"Hey, look at us! We're already bonding."

I can't help but laugh. "Bonding over laundry. Great."

Josh smiles at my honest laughter. I could get lost in that smile. His eyes. I notice that the brown splatter in his eye looks much lighter today, almost hazel. It's so unique. I wonder what caused this slight genetic mutation. A beautiful one, at that. Would it be weird to ask? I know we only just reunited, but I already hunger to know more about him.

"Oh, right. I got you a gift," Josh says as he reaches out to hand me the bag. "It's nothing much really. Saw it and thought of you."

As I reach out for the bag, a wave of cold dread washes over me. I hate opening gifts in front of people. Loathe it. There's too much pressure to react in such a way that validates both the giver and receiver, like with cards. Suppressing this societal disdain, I force an appreciative smile, open the bag, and look inside. All I see is a bottle of Coke, a bag of Cheetos, a bottle of sunscreen, and a card.

I close the bag and look over at Josh with a confused smirk. "Hm…interesting…"

"Remember that receipt I wrote my number on the last time I was here? It was for a Coke and a bag of Cheetos. I figured, hey, best to play it safe."

"I see…but what's with the sunscreen though?"

Josh shrugs. "Well, in the card is a gift certificate to a floating obstacle course on Lake Otto. I was hoping you'd want to go there with me for a second date. Kate mentioned that you burn easy."

"So, that's what this is, huh?" I counter. "A first date? And when did you talk to Kate?"

"She texted me the other day to let me know that my background check had cleared. Whatever that means. And yes, I would consider this a date."

I thought for a moment before asking, "And how did my proclivity to sunburns come up in this conversation between you and Kate?"

"I told her if I got lucky enough to take you on a second date that I'd want to take you to the lake. Kate said you would love that but would need to bring sunscreen."

I love Kate. I love that she acts like this super hard, judgmental person, but, in reality, isn't that at all. She knows how difficult it is for me to bounce back from a manic phase—a situation only made riskier by adding a new relationship to the mix. I know she's worried about me. She's conflicted. Conflicted by the want for me to be happy, with or without an intimate partner. Hell, I'm conflicted too. By doing a background check on Josh, I know she must like him. She sees his potential for good. This is just a way to ease her mind, to know I'm probably in safe hands.

"Don't worry; Kate means well," I say. "She's all I have and just wants to make sure I don't end up getting hurt."

Without hesitation, Josh looks into my eyes and says,

"Sarah, you're fascinatingly mysterious to me. Trust me when I say that I have no intention of hurting you. Ever." He pauses slightly before chuckling. "Wow, that came out weird. Sorry, I'm a little nervous."

Sarcastically, I say, "Yeah, I tend to have that effect on people."

Josh laughs. "Oh no, you don't make me nervous. Kate, on the other hand…"

Together, we laugh.

I hate to say it, but I'm falling hard for this guy. From my head down to my toes, I can feel a fuzzy warmness crawling its way through me. I look at him and feel so much happiness. I try hard to differentiate between my manic thought process and my real feelings, but it's no easy feat. I have trouble finding the words to describe exactly how I feel. Only one word comes close: *safe*. Josh makes me feel *safe*.

Pulling me back out from inside myself, I hear Josh casually ask, "Ready to head out?"

"Let's do this!" Genuinely excited for what the day might bring, we head toward the front door.

As we enter Sedona, I spot a series of massive red rocks. They seem to be meticulously sculpted into the landscape— monolithic globs of dried clay, left behind by forgotten giants. The sight alone is breathtaking. This rare geological beauty is hard for me to fully comprehend. Overwhelmed, I can't help but turn my head to look away. This is when I notice Josh. He has one hand gripping the steering wheel, the other resting on his knee. He looks poised in that moment, totally calm and collected. As I'm admiring this stoic display,

Josh looks over and catches me staring. His first reaction is a smooth smile, subtle but warm. Even though he doesn't come right out and say it, I can tell that he's much more relaxed now compared to when we were back at my apartment. Two hours of forced conversation in a speeding vehicle can do that, I'm sure.

On the drive, we chatted a little bit about his job. Apparently, Josh owns a small drywall company. We talked about his parents and four siblings. He has two older sisters and two younger brothers. Josh is the middle child. Unlucky bastard. His oldest sister, Grace, is thirty-six. The second oldest sister, Anne, is thirty-three. According to Josh, he's closest to Anne; they're barely a year apart in age. Anne was only a month old when her mother got pregnant with Josh. He was one of those surprise babies. The two younger brothers, Aaron and Alen, are twins. At only twenty-one years old, they sit far on the opposite end of the age gap.

Aaron and Alen are both in college. Both of them are avid baseball players, and pretty damn good at it. On their way to the major leagues, by the way Josh tells it. His oldest sister, Grace, holds some position in the legal field. I can't remember what exactly. But of all his siblings, Josh talked about Anne the most. She seems kind and gentle, yet very protective of Josh. I wonder if I'll get to meet her someday.

Josh's mom and dad are still married. They had their first child, Grace, when they were both only eighteen years old, barely graduated from high school. With not a lot of job options, Josh's dad enlisted in the military. In the meantime, Josh's mom graduated college in between birthing two more children—Anne and Josh. Even though she got her degree,

Josh's mother never chose to work outside the home. I guess parenting was a bigger priority.

During the long drive, I tried to keep Josh talking about his own life and family. Whenever he would break away to ask about me, I would find a way to redirect the question. The timeless art of deflection. I just don't want him to know certain things about me. Is that wrong? It's all so embarrassing. I don't want to scare him away with horror stories of how dysfunctional my family was. My childhood was rooted in addiction and abuse—ruled by a parent with a severe mental health disorder. Not exactly glamorous by any stretch of the imagination. I know Josh wouldn't understand. From his own account, he has the perfect family. The perfect life.

Before I know it, we're pulling up to a building. As Josh parks the car, I unbuckle my seatbelt and glance out my side window to see a Jeep with *Sedona Guided Tours* scrawled across the side in big white letters. Side by side, Josh and I cross the parking lot together. Our stride abruptly stops when I notice that there's a note on the building's front door that reads,

<u>BY RESERVATION ONLY</u>
<u>No walk-ins</u>

This is when I feel an icy shiver of fear run through me. I got so excited at the idea of spending time with Josh that I never made the stupid reservation!

When I falter to open the door and step inside, Josh senses my hesitation and asks, "Is everything okay?" Before I can muddle together an answer, he leans in closer to read the sign on the door. "Reservation only, huh? That's kind of silly."

I can tell that he has a sense of what's happening but is trying not to call me out directly. He knows I dropped the ball. Big time.

Turning from the door, Josh smiles and says, "Oh well. No big deal. We'll just have to find something else to do."

"I'm so sorry," I groan, face redder than those clay mountains. "I must've missed that part on the paper. God, so stupid of me." I say this knowing damn well that I probably did read that part and just totally forgot about it. Like an idiot.

"Maybe we can save the tour for our third date," Josh says. "How does that sound?"

"My my, such confidence."

"Hey, it's still cool for friends to go on platonic dates, right?"

"Maybe? Can't say I've ever been on one though."

"Well, if it's alright with you, we can call this our first platonic date."

Jokingly, I retort, "Hey, it's your funeral."

Never missing my wit, Josh immediately laughs. "Sweet. Let's go."

Former plans now derailed; we soon head off on foot. To where, only Josh knows. Right away, I see that the streets are lined with tourists and open shops. As we move through the never-ending crowd of looky-loos, I wonder, *Does he feel what I'm feeling? Or am I just imagining this? What if this thing between us goes even further? When should I tell him about...you know? Hell, should I even tell him at all? What will he say if I do? I can't even begin to imagine…*

Keeping my cool, I push all my worries to the back of my brain—compartmentalizing them—and continue to stroll at Josh's side. More than anything, I'm determined to enjoy this day. No matter what.

LOVE AND CHAOS
CHAPTER 6

I woke up just before sunrise, the first long rays of sunshine barely touching my bedroom window. Normally, I sleep in a little bit, but my mind has been racing non-stop for most of the night and early morning. I just can't lay here with my eyes shut any longer. Lying in bed, I try to imagine all the people who are just now waking up to start their day.

How many of them are having sex right now? How many are crying? Laughing? How many of them are cheating on their partners?

Slowly, I roll over in bed to face Josh. He's still fast asleep. I quietly admire how peaceful he looks. Picturesque. I watch his chest rise and fall with each soft breath. Like a flock of birds flying past a closed window shade, I can see his eyes darting back and forth under his eyelids. His shirt is off, revealing a tattoo of an otter on the left side of his chest. Right over his heart. When I asked him about the tattoo, Josh told me that it was some dumb thing that he and his friends agreed to do. Each one chose the animal that they felt best represented them. Most of his friends chose something overly macho like a bear, lion, or shark for their tattoo. Not Josh though. Of all the beasts in the animal kingdom he could've picked, he chose the otter. Which, when I thought about it, makes total sense. As I lie here, lightly tracing my fingers over the tattoo, I think about how similar Josh is to an otter. He's soft, curious, and generally nice when not threatened. Both strong and protective. I look back up at his resting face and can see that he's in a very deep sleep.

After two months of dating exclusively, I decided last night that Josh would stay over at my place for the first time. Well, technically not the *first* time, but I don't count my last birthday. Kate was here with us for the whole night, so, naturally, nothing sexual transpired. The first time we had sex was at his parents' house about a month ago—only a few weeks after our trip to Sedona.

With Easter coming up fast, Josh had asked me if I would be interested in flying to Oregon with him to meet his family. Although neither he nor his family are religious types, the Easter holiday get together is something they all took very seriously. And since I've always wanted to visit Oregon, I agreed to go. A part of me also needed to see if Josh's family was as "normal" as he portrayed them to be.

Once our plane landed in Oregon, we got a rental car and headed straight to his parents' place. The drive there was like something out of *Lord of the Rings*. The long road ahead seemed to wind endlessly through a green abyss of dense forests and luscious valleys. Above, a quilted pillowtop of dark, fluffy clouds misted everything in fine dew. When we eventually turned off the main road and onto a dirt driveway, my jaw immediately dropped.

Tucked about a half mile up the hill was a beautiful two-story log cabin. Like something ripped from an old oil painting, tendrils of white smoke bellowed from the cabins' tall brick chimney. I watched the smoke rise before being quickly consumed by the passing wind. The wraparound porch, still dark with lacquer, reached all the way up to the second story. Truly, a sight to be held. As Josh put the car in park, all I could do was just sit there and admire the whole scene. Totally awestruck. In my mind, this was a place where you'd find magical fairies and trolls—not Middle Earth but close enough. A place wholly untouched by the dark evils of the mechanical world.

Or at least that's what I imagined.

Still sitting in the car, I watched as the cabin's front door suddenly opened, and a line of people started filing outside. As Josh opened his car door to climb out, he first leaned over to me and whispered, "You good?"

Stiffly, I smiled and nodded. "Yeah…I'm good." As soon as Josh exited the car, a woman ran forward from the group and tackled him to the ground. Dumbfounded, I stepped out to watch them playfully wrestle on the ground. What was happening? I watched as Josh easily out muscled the woman, quickly gaining control. Like a prize fighter mocking his opponent for the bloodthirsty crowd, he sat on the woman's stomach and started tickling her sides. Soon, they were both laughing hysterically.

From the open front door of the cabin, an older woman emerged to yell, "Knock it off, you two!"

"Josh, stop! She's gonna pee her pants!" one of the men on the porch added.

"Let her!" another woman chimed in. "That's what she gets!"

"Who's your favorite brother?" Josh teasingly asked the woman, still pinning her down to tickle her sides.

In between big whoops of laughter, the woman blurted

out, "You are! You are! Now, stop it! Please!"

Seconds later, Josh stood back up. He offered his hand to help the woman up, but when he did, she skillfully kicked his feet out from under him, causing Josh to drop to the ground like a stone. With grass in her hair and mud smearing her pants, the woman sprang back up to her feet and loomed over Josh. Examining the deep tear in the left shoulder of her shirt, she glared down at him and hissed, "Ah, you still suck. See, I didn't even pee my pants."

Admitting slight defeat, Josh smiled and slowly stood back up. I watched as he gave the girl a big hug and then whispered something in her ear. The woman then turned around and gave me a big, welcoming smile. As she approached, she attempted to casually shake the loose mud and grass from her hair. When I noticed she wasn't slowing her pace, I came to a shocking realization:

Oh no…she's going to hug me!

Just as I had predicted, the woman walked right up and wrapped her arms around me. Tight, too. "Sarah! I'm so glad to finally meet you!" As quickly as it began, the hug was over. No harm, no foul. "Damn, I'm so sorry," the woman suddenly added. "Josh warned me you weren't a hugger. Sorry, I forgot."

Evenly, not letting my annoyance show, I relaxed my shoulders and awkwardly smiled. "No, it's okay. You're fine."

"I'm Anne," she said, taking a step back so we could shake hands.

"Oh, nice to meet you, Anne. Josh has told me so much about you."

I was taken aback by how beautiful Anne is. She's like the

female version of Josh. Her eyes are a solid green though, no spots or blemishes. Her skin, nicely tanned, perfectly accents her straight brown hair. I noticed that she has very full lips, and a small freckle in the outer corner of her right eye. She's much taller than I imagined, at least four inches taller than I am. Just as Josh said, Anne radiated a strong aura of warmth and love. Seeing her smile made me want to smile. It was infectious. I could very easily see why she was Josh's favorite sibling.

Anne, now turned back to Josh, said, "You're right; she does have super soft hands."

At those words, Josh's face goes totally blank. Blushing, he shouts back, "Anne, come on! I told you that in confidence, man!"

I couldn't help but laugh. I wondered how much he's told her about me. Does she know that I have bipolar? I decided to fess up to Josh during our trip to Sedona. I figured it'd be better if he knew sooner rather than later. I knew that my bipolar could be a real deal breaker, especially if I sprang it on him later in the game. I wanted him to know early on before things got too deep between us. Are you in or out? Well, when I told Josh, he didn't really seem to care. Go figure.

Joining us by the car, Josh teasingly added, "Are you hitting on my girlfriend, Anne?"

"Whoa, girlfriend?!" another woman commented. From the porch, the same woman waved at me. "Hi, I'm Grace! The older, wiser sister! Nice to meet you, Sarah!"

Blushing, I sheepishly waved back. To be honest, I didn't know what Josh and I were at the time. He hadn't asked me to be his girlfriend and I hadn't asked him to be my boyfriend. It was like we were in a relationship limbo. I hadn't been in a serious relationship for so long that I forgot how awkward all this was. I know I'm 100% exclusive with Josh, so I just assumed that he was exclusive with me too. Still, probably wouldn't hurt to get further clarification on the matter.

Amongst all the chatter, I noticed Josh had a big cheesy smile on his face. He's normally such a chill person, but he seemed even more relaxed than ever. Suddenly, he looked at me and said, "I'll grab our stuff real quick from the trunk." As he headed around the car, he stopped to gently kiss me on the forehead. Smiling, he leaned in close and whispered, "I'm so glad you're here."

On the porch stood two men who looked eerily similar. By the power of deduction, I figured this must be the twins—Aaron and Alen.

"Hey, Big J!" one of them yelled to Josh. "You need a hand over there?!"

"Nah, I got it!" Josh yelled back. "Thanks, Aaron!"

"It's Alen, dumbass!"

Josh, popping his head back out of the trunk, squinted his eyes and grinned. "Ah, nice try, Aaron! I may be getting old, but I'm not blind!"

Still on the porch, Aaron and Alen shared a laugh. Honestly, I couldn't tell them apart. Like Siamese cats, they were vertically identical in every single way. Their facial structure, build and even smiles were exactly the same. They both used their hands a lot as they talked too. Their hair was even swooped to the same side.

When Aaron caught me examining him and his brother like they were zebras at the Zoo, he hitched a thumb over at Alen and joked, "He has a birthmark on his left butt cheek. I don't."

Unsure of how to respond to hearing such information, I stifled a laugh and said, "Nice to meet you both."

Suddenly, an older woman stepped forward, cutting through the crowd to join us down by the car. "Sarah, we're so glad you made it." She gestured back to the twins. "Please excuse my feral children over there. I'm Joan." Nodding to the third man standing on the porch, she added, "And that's Steve."

"Hi, Sarah!" Steve called out to me. "I've got a bum leg or else I'd come down there to introduce myself."

I felt like I was standing in some weird fever dream. As if, at any moment, they would all pull their faces off and start chasing me through the woods.

REAL families don't actually act like this…do they?

Looking to the sky, Joan said, "Rains pickin' up. Better come on in the house. You're bound to catch a cold standing out here in this drizzle."

Through all the love and chaos, I didn't even notice that the slight misting had measurably thickened. As everyone filed back into the cabin, I stayed behind to look up at the sky. On the distant horizon, ancient fir trees stood as tall as skyscrapers. Their pointed tops swayed back and forth, feathered fingers tickling fresh rain from the darkened clouds. I could hear the wind whispering between them, speaking the language of the Earth. As I closed my eyes and took a deep breath inward, I could hear the distant creaking of tree branches. Soon, my face was drenched—covering me in rogue tears of summer rain.

"Sarah, you coming in?!" Josh yelled to me from the porch.

When I opened my eyes, everyone was gone. I stood alone in the yard while Josh stood on the porch. I had no idea how long I'd been standing there for. Could have been seconds or hours. Reminding myself how amazing this all was, I turned around and followed Josh inside.

As I entered the cabin, I saw a steep wooden staircase that led straight up to a wide-open balcony space. The outer edge of the balcony was decorated in festive hanging pots and plants. To the left of the staircase was the kitchen doorway—to the right, the living room. Directly behind the staircase was a long hallway lined with bedrooms and maybe a bathroom.

As Josh set our luggage down by the staircase, I heard Joan holler, "Dinner's done, guys! Come get it!"

The food smelled amazing. Passing through the kitchen and into the dining room, Josh and I soon joined the rest of the family at a large dining table—something my family never did. Not even once.

I stayed mostly silent throughout the dinner, covertly observing how Josh's family interacted with each other. I watched them laugh, share stories, and playfully argue about sports. Seeing all this left me with only two assumptions: either they were the most normal family I'd ever met, or an amazing group of method actors.

After dinner, Joan told the kids to clean up so she could show Josh and I to our room upstairs. I offered to help Josh carry some of our bags, but he flat out refused. I know, such chivalry.

As I walked up the stairs ahead of Josh, I took the time to examine several framed pictures that hung on the staircase wall. Most of them were old school and youth sports photos. One by one, I took them in with passing intrigue as we ascended to the second-floor balcony. Once at the top of the stairs, we came to the head of a long hallway. There were four doors in all: one on the left side, two on the right, and one at the end.

We followed Joan down the hallway to the first door on the right. Upon entering the room, I was shocked. With a single bed set against the left wall, my eye was immediately drawn to the giant set of sliding glass doors that led out to a spacious balcony. Slowly, I walked across the room to the sliding doors and peered outward. For miles and miles ahead was nothing but a green sea of treetops. Even farther in the distance, shrouded in a floating veil of rain and fog, was the lumbering silhouette of a mighty mountain range.

"Out there is Mount St. Helens, Mount Rainier, and Mount Hood," Joan said factually. "Breathtaking, aren't they?" Even from behind fog and glass, I could see their dusty white caps of virgin white snow. With a sigh of relief, she added, "Yup, gotta love that view. I wanted to make sure you and Josh got the best room in the house."

"Mom, come on," Josh anxiously sighed. "I specifically asked you not to do this."

Without skipping a beat, Joan turned to Josh and said, "Oh, relax. It's no problem. Besides, the floors in that other room are in the middle of being redone and nobody's allowed in there. Well, goodnight, you two." Before Josh could argue any further, Joan slipped out of the room, shut the door, and headed back downstairs.

Shrugging off all our luggage onto the floor, Josh gave me an apologetic look and said, "I'm sorry. I blatantly asked her not to stick us in the same room like this. If you want, you can stay here and I can grab my bags and just sleep on the couch downstairs."

"No, no, that's okay. Besides, why would I mind? I'm your girlfriend, remember?"

At first, Josh didn't say anything. Expression dire, he looked me in the eye and asked, "So…you're serious then? You really want to be my girlfriend?"

At a loss for words, I leave the balcony doors and take a seat at the edge of the bed. "What about…the whole *bipolar* thing?"

"Huh? What about the bipolar thing?" he asked with genuine confusion.

"I'm serious, Josh. You don't know how bad it can get sometimes. You…you can't know…" I tried my best to warn him, but no words would suffice.

"You're right…I don't know, but I'm more than willing to learn. I want to know everything about you, Sarah. Bipolar is only a small percentage of who you are as a person. It doesn't define you."

Shocked to tears, I silently looked away, shamed by my own sense of self-loathing. I listened as Josh then crossed the room and got down on one knee at the edge of the bed. Gently, he reached out and raised my chin until our eyes met once again.

"The last few weeks with you have been amazing," he said. "And I want more. I want more of *you*, Sarah. I want more of...*this*. Whatever *this* may be."

There it was, that spark. In a matter of seconds, it drew us together into a passionate kiss. When our lips touched, I felt my entire body soften like wax under a flame. It was as if I had been locked in an emotional stasis of sorts. I couldn't remember the last time my mind was so quiet, so barren of negative energy. I was totally immersed in the moment, only needing to feel the weight of his body resting against mine.

Slowly, Josh pulled away from our kiss. Still sitting at the edge of the bed, I lifted my gaze to meet his but stopped halfway. I heard myself sharply gasp as my hungry eyes traced the bulging outline of Josh's hard cock. Realizing what I was staring at, Josh slightly blushed and attempted to cover himself with his hands. But I wouldn't allow it. Before he could shy away, I reached up, grabbed the waist of his jeans, and yanked him forward. As Josh tumbled on top of me, I leaned back and embraced him—legs spread and arms reaching. In between receiving a flutter of small kisses along the nape of my neck, I yanked Josh's shirt off over his head. Once free, he rose to his knees, allowing me to unbuckle his pants.

When he stood up from the bed to remove his underwear, I couldn't help but admire his amazing physique. My eyes started all the way at the top and slowly worked their way down scanning every naked inch of him. He was flawless. When my eyes finally reached his still hard member, I was at a loss for words. I haven't been with that many guys before Josh, but his tool was by far the largest I'd ever seen. I was surprised to see that he was completely clean shaven, with just the slightest shade of stubble.

Suddenly, Josh snapped his fingers and said, "Oh, hold on. Wait right there just a second." He rummaged through his jeans for his wallet. Taking out two unused condoms from an inside flap, he walked over and set them both on the bedside table.

All I can remember thinking at that moment was how badly I wanted him inside of me. More than I've ever wanted anything else before. Heart pounding in anticipation, I watched him stroll back over to the bed. With delicate care, he then started unbuttoning my jeans. I decided to help him along by shucking my pants off in one fluent motion. Josh couldn't help but laugh at this. I knew it wasn't smart to show all my cards like this, but I didn't care anymore. I needed him badly. Still riding that wave of euphoric lust, I tore off my shirt and threw it to the floor with the rest of our clothes.

"May I?" Josh asked, gesturing to my bra and panties.

"Yes, please."

I leaned back as Josh pulled down my panties and tossed them to the floor. Sensually, he then parted my legs and began lightly kissing down the inside of my thighs. With each soft kiss, I felt his hot lips moving closer and closer. And just as he's about to put his mouth on my slit, I quickly sat up and gasped, "Whoa, wait a minute."

"I'm sorry," Josh immediately responded, pulling back. I could hear the worry in his voice. "Did I do something wrong?"

"No. It's just…uhm…what're you doing?"

Josh paused for a moment, as if he didn't understand what I was asking. "Uh…just a little bit of foreplay, I guess. That's all, I swear."

"Like…with your mouth?"

Josh couldn't help but chuckle at my ignorance. "Well, yeah. Is that okay?"

Anxiously, I tucked my knees up to my chest. "I've actually never…uhm…never had anyone do that before."

"Oh…" I could tell by the look on his face that he was surprised by my confession. And before I could mumble my way through an excuse, Josh coyly smiled and asked, "Would you…would you want to try?"

For obvious reasons, I didn't have to think over the proposition for very long. "Yeah, I think I would. But could I freshen up first? All this traveling has made me feel kinda dirty."

Josh flashed me another million-dollar smile and said, "Totally understandable. The bathroom is over there. Take your time."

Bouncing to my feet, I get on my tiptoes to get another kiss from Josh before skittering away to the bathroom. Once inside, I did a quick sniff test of my lady bits. All was good on that front. Feeling confident, I left the bathroom and lay back down on the bed.

I could feel my body shaking with feral excitement. Although I was mentally ready, I had never felt so nervous about anything in my whole entire life. Josh could tell that I was nervous too; he held back at first. Tentatively, he traced his fingers along the fine curves of my body—traveling along my navel and up around my breasts. I could feel my skin rising with goosebumps as he continued to touch me with utmost care. Without a word, Josh stealthily reached back and unhooked my bra. Soon, his mouth was on my hard nipples, wet tongue lapping and lips sucking. The sensation caused me to shiver with ecstasy.

Josh stopped to look up at me. Eyes locked, he whispered, "You still okay with this?"

Lost in the moment, all I could do was bite my bottom lip and nod.

...I'm all yours...

Sensually, leaving a trail of wet kisses down my torso, Josh spread my thighs apart and pressed his warm tongue against my throbbing clit. I could feel every flick and turn, the heat of his tongue sliding in and around me. In that moment, I felt like I was having an out of body experience. Detached but still wholly there. The sheer level of pleasure coursing through me was surreal, as if a hidden door had been opened up somewhere deep inside. Fingering me slowly with one hand, Josh used the other to reach up and tease my hard, pink nipples. Like a birthday balloon, I felt my brain swell with inertial ecstasy. Every eager wag of his tongue, every slow turn of his fingers, brought me closer and closer to the edge.

Then, just when I thought my head might explode, I came.

In that moment, I felt as though our souls had intertwined—metaphysically fused together to form one being. Although my eyes were open, my vision was blinded by brilliant flashes of white light and shooting stars. I thought I wanted this, but, in actuality, I *needed* it.

Melted to the bed, I lazily watched as Josh got up to retrieve one of the condoms from the bedside table. As he tore the wrapper open and slid the condom over his stiff cock, he looked down at me and asked, "You sure you're ready for this? No pressure if you aren't."

Still riding the high of that last incredible orgasm, I just smiled and nodded in response. I was ready. Dragging my shivering body over to the foot of the bed, Josh gently spread my legs back open and slid himself inside. But only a little at first. I gasped, eyes wide and fingers clenching the sheets, as he eased the rest in. Slowly, Josh rocked his hips, rhythmically thrusting in and out. In and out. I watched his chest flex with each long thrust—muscles taught. His eyes never once left my face. When he knelt forward to kiss me again, I reached up and ran my fingers through his hair. He was driving me crazy. As Josh kissed me harder, the rhythm of his hips gradually quickened. Faster and faster, I felt myself reaching the edge again. Face hot, lips swollen with blood, I moaned and threw myself back against the bed as another earth-shattering orgasm rippled through me. Bodies now in perfect harmony, Josh also climaxed in that moment. Our eyes locked, heavy beads of sweat mingling with gracious tears. We were riding the same wave, a shared momentum unlike anything I'd ever experienced before. Once it was over, Josh pulled out and slowly wilted down next to me on the bed. Hand in hand, we lay there—nothing in the room but our labored breathing and tangled heartbeats. I wanted that moment to last forever. It was...*perfect*.

As Josh sat up and stepped down from the bed, I

dreamily rolled my head to the side and groaned, "Well…does this make us official?"

Still naked, he turned to me, scratched his chin, and said, "Hm…nope. I don't think so." Before I could express my confusion, Josh reached down and fished out a small, folded piece of paper from one of his jeans' pockets and handed it to me. I unfolded the paper to find a bunch of scribbled notes, some scratched out entirely.

Sarah, can we take our relationship to the next level?
Do you wanna go out with me exclusively?
Sarah, will you be my girlfriend?
Can we be exclusive?
Can we talk about making this official?

"I've been trying to figure out just the right way to ask," Josh admitted. "I've literally been waiting since the night we got home from Sedona to do it." Laughing, he shrugged and added, "This isn't how I imagined it going down but…Sarah, will you be my girlfriend?"

I smiled. "Yes, I will. so…*now* are we official?"

"Yeah…we're official…"

Looking back on that trip, there's no doubt in my mind that it was a life-changing experience for me. With Josh still sleeping at my side, I roll back over in bed and observe the now sunbaked window. Even in these early morning hours, my apartment feels eerily quiet. Almost too calm.

A few minutes later, just as I felt myself starting to drift off again into another past-time fantasy, I hear a voice from over my shoulder say, "Good mornin', beautiful."

I roll back over to see Josh rubbing the last bits of sleep from his eyes. "Good morning."

"How long have you been awake?"

I shrug. "A while."

Josh smiles and gently kisses my forehead. "Staying in bed to daydream a little?

"Yeah, something like that. Hey…you remember the first time we had sex?"

"Of course, I do. Why you ask?"

"I was just wondering…do you always carry condoms around with you?"

Josh, pausing to evaluate my question, smirkingly responds, "Yeah, just in case. Better to be safe than sorry, ya know?"

This answer makes me slightly uneasy. "Uh-huh. So, you just carry them around with you? To use with *who* exactly? To use with me…or someone else?" Sensing the building tension between us, Josh quickly sits up in bed. Now totally awake, he flashes me a weary look, unsure of how to proceed. "Were you sleeping with somebody else when we first hooked up?" I ask directly.

"No," Josh is quick to answer. "I just thought, since we were getting so close, that there was a possibility that we might sleep together on the trip. I wanted to be prepared. I'm sorry, I know it was probably wrong of me to assume that."

Josh doesn't know it, but this is the initiating process of what I like to call Phase 4. Severe paranoia and petty insecurities are a huge part of Phase 4. But even worse than Phase 4 is Phase 5. And if I don't get a handle on myself now, the consequences could be deadly.

Reluctantly, I sigh, "Look, I'm sorry. I didn't mean to start anything. I'm just not feeling great this morning. Might need some time alone for a little bit. Nothing personal."

"I would never hurt you, Sarah," Josh further insists. I can tell he's freaked out by my accusations, but I just don't feel like explaining myself right now. It's all way too much to dive into first thing in the morning.

"I know you wouldn't," I say with my tone getting louder, "but this is what I've been trying to warn you about. I...I can't have love without chaos."

I can feel my heart starting to race, my chest tightening. I roll over and reach for my phone on the nightstand. As fresh beads of sweat start to sprout from my skin, I find Kate's number and call. The whole time I'm doing this, I can feel Josh curiously watching me from over my shoulder. This is making this worse. His stares are cutting through me.

After a few short rings, Kate answers the call. "Hello? Sarah?" I don't know how, but I can tell by her voice that she already knows something's wrong.

"Kate...I...uhm..." That's all I have to say.

"Say no more; I'm on my way," is Kate's immediate response. "Just stay on the phone with me and don't hang up. Is Josh still there?"

I had told her last night that Josh was staying over. I'm glad I did. At the mention of his name, I look over and see that he's still watching me from his side of the bed. I don't want Josh to see me like this. Christ, I'd done so well to hide it too. So much for all that. I take a moment to look around at my studio apartment. It's small, but for some reason feels way smaller. The accusatory voices and feelings in my head make the walls close in even tighter. And with the two of us crammed in here, it's getting really hard to breathe.

"Sarah?" I hear Josh say. "Do you need me to—"

"Just fuckin' leave!" I erupt, practically snarling at him. "Don't look at me! Just get the fuck out of here! Right now! Go!"

Stunned by my outburst, Josh jumps up from the bed and slowly backs out of the room. "Okay okay, I'll leave…"

It kills me to see that look of pain and confusion in his eyes. I can tell that I've hurt him. So much so, that I'm afraid he might start crying. Like a tarnished prisoner, I watch as he hurriedly puts his pants, shirt, socks, and shoes on. As he grabs his wallet off the kitchen counter, he then turns back to face me.

"I'm not sure what I did wrong…but I just want you to know that I'm still here for you, Sarah. Just let me know and I'll be there." Josh then turns back for the hallway and disappears. When I hear the sound of the front door opening, then latching shut again, I finally allow myself to cry.

Realizing that I'm still gripping the phone, I sobbingly bring it up to my ear and say, "Kate, I…I think I lost him."

"Sarah, I want you to do me a favor," Kate sternly says. "I want you to focus on specific objects around you. Can you do this? Tell me, what do you see? Take your time and don't forget to breathe."

Kate isn't focusing on my love drama; she's focusing on keeping me here, in the present.

Taking a deep, shaky breath, I wipe the blur of tears from

my eyes nad look around my apartment. "Okay…I see the carpet. The T.V. Some laundry. Uhm…I see the table…the curtains…"

DECEPTION
CHAPTER 7

Although I can feel the sun peeking in through my bedroom window, cooking my exposed skin, I still don't want to get out of bed. Instead, I sink deeper into the mattress. Soon, the bed and I are one. I imagine myself disintegrating. Like grains of sand, my body sifts through the threads of my sheets and disappears. It's been a week since I flipped out on Josh, and I still feel pretty shitty about it. When I feel the rough vibration of my phone from under the pillow, I dig it out and take a look. There's four missed calls and thirteen unread text messages—all from Josh and Kate.

I missed the cues, I tell myself. *How could I let this happen? I feel like a total failure. Oh well, it doesn't matter now. Nothing does. Josh and I had a good run…but now it's over. Done. All I can do now is sink deeper, all the way down until I reach that thin line between life and death. I feel so betrayed by…well…by myself. I fucked up bad this time…*

Technically speaking, I still have a chance to pull myself back out of this. But once I've crossed over into Phase 5—the "crash" phase—I'll lose all sense of logic. The intrusive thoughts—the noise, the guilt—will eventually take over. My only hope now is to find my way through to the other side before it's too late.

As I stare blankly into space, stranded in a cavernous pit

of despair, I feel my phone vibrate again. Too morose to even look at it, I let the phone fall from my hand, tumble off the edge of the bed, and clatter to the floor.

If I don't look at it, I reason, *then no one can accuse me of ghosting them…*

Suddenly, I hear the familiar sound of keys jangling at my front door. I should've known better than to ignore Kate's calls; now she's here to confront me in person.

As the front door creaks open, I hear Kate worryingly call out, "Sarah?! Sarah, are you here?!"

Barely moving, I lift my head and drearily reply, "Yeah, I'm back here."

I manage to sit myself up in bed when Kate comes racing around the corner to the bedroom. I feel so ashamed, I can't even look her in the eye as she slowly approaches the bed. I can't stand to see her so worried, so torn up inside over some stupid shit that I pulled. It isn't fair, all the unnecessary stress that I cause her. I just want to disappear. I hate myself for ever allowing anyone to get this close to me. Like a sinking ship, I can't help but drag them under.

Nervously, I start picking at my nails as Kate walks over and grabs my phone off the floor. I finally look up to see that she has a duffel bag slung over one shoulder.

"Sarah, why?" Kate asks as she angrily scrolls through the notifications on my phone. Her tone is thick with frustration and concern.

The question is moot; Kate knows exactly what's going on. I'm sure she was secretly hoping that her gut feeling about me was wrong, but it wasn't. On a subconscious level, I know that this one is deep. It's going to require a large amount of energy and determination to pull me out of the rut I'm in. The work required seems insurmountable. Kate can hope all she wants that this will simply go away, but that's all just wishful thinking.

We both know where this shitstorm is heading.

"Jesus, Sarah," Kate added. "Don't even act like you didn't see all these calls and texts I sent you."

I groan. "Please, don't start with this. I don't need your judgement right now. Why don't you go find a new friend to play phone tag with then?"

I regret the words before I'm even done speaking. How could I treat my best friend so terribly, especially after everything she's done for me? It makes no sense. I just want to suffer alone, free from the added guilt of taking some innocent soul down with me. I admit; it's easier for me to lash out than to be vulnerable. Even so, pushing Kate away never works. She'll stick it out with me. No matter what.

"When *we* get through this," Kate says. "I'm 100% going to revisit that bullshit comment. Don't you worry."

…Fair enough…

Although Kate's words are strong, her expression is one of immense hurt and sadness. Normally bright eyes now cloudy with tears, hair unbrushed and tattered, she looks thoroughly exhausted. Drained. I know Kate deserves better than this. She doesn't deserve all the bullshit I've been putting her through.

"Please, just let me go through this alone, Kate," I beg. Although I don't really want to do this alone, I can't stand to watch her suffer too. Like wearing a corset made of shameful guilt, my chest feels uncomfortably tight. Restricted. My hands shake uncontrollably. I hate everything about myself.

Why am I even here? Why am I even alive? Is this the rest of my life? Cursed to bring down every else around me. A human sinkhole of negativity. More than anything, I don't want this.

The thought of spending the rest of my life in this stupid limbo makes me want to go to sleep and never wake up again.

When Kate drops the duffel bag onto the bed, I look up to see that she's smiling. I watch her unzip the bag, pull out her PJ's, and hold them up to me. We jokingly call the outfit her moo-moo movie shirt—a hideous long shirt with a giant cartoon cactus plastered on the front. Along with that, Kate also brought some chips, candy, and sodas for us to share. I giggle at the sodas; when I'm depressed, I refuse to drink alcohol. So does Kate. So, we drink our weight in soda instead. Lastly, she reaches into the bag and pulls out my favorite movie trilogy *The Lord of the Rings*. Whenever I get like this I for some reason, watch *The Lord of the Rings* over and over. Kate willingly does it with me.

"Today," Kate confidently announces, "we're going to ignore the outside world, eat too much junk food, and watch movies. But only if we spend tomorrow making a plan. Agreed?"

Disgraced, I lower my eyes and nod in agreement. It's an empty promise, and we both know it. There I am, hanging from the edge of a hypothetical cliff. Without the strength to pull myself back up, the only way I can go from here is down. That is, unless Kate is there to pull me back up to my feet. She knows that when I get depressed, it's easy for me to get lost in my own thoughts.

In a flash, Kate strips off her shirt and jeans and slides into her baggy overnight shirt. As if donning a beautiful ballgown, she twirls and does a curtsy at the foot of the bed. I feel a genuine giggle bubble up inside my chest. We look at each other and laugh, somehow putting us both at ease.

Since my T.V. and DVD player are on a moveable stand, Kate wastes no time wheeling the whole thing over so we can watch movies in bed. After putting in the first of many discs, she leaps into bed and nestles in at my side. Kate opens the first bag of goodies and holds them out to me. Cheetos—one of my culinary weaknesses. I just can't get enough of that powdery, cheesy goodness. Unable to say no, I reach into the bag and grab a healthy handful. I didn't realize just how hungry I was until I started eating them. When I finish the handful and start to suck the cheese off my fingertips, I catch Kate scoping me from the corner of her eye.

"You're not hungry, huh? Yeah, okay." Kate smirks, voice laced with thick sarcasm. Acting in the moment, I casually turn and drag my cheesy fingers down the right sleeve of her shirt. "Ugh, Sarah! Gross!"

I can't help but laugh as I say, "Hold onto that for me please. Thanks."

Joining me in my laughter, Kate suddenly leans over and gives me a big hug. No words. She wraps her arms around my shoulders and squeezes me so tight that I struggle to catch my breath. I cough, cheese dust now clotting in my throat. Weakly, I stop fighting her touch and submit. I have no other choice but to hug her back. Nothing needs to be said; we both have our own reasons for sharing this sacred bond. For Kate, the hug helps to quiet the nagging worry she sometimes feels for me. I need the hug simply because Kate needs it. That's it. I can't stand to see her in pain.

Soon, the hug ends, and Kate pulls away to continue watching the movie. As she nestles back down into her seat, my eyes continue to linger, carefully watching her at my side.

How was I ever so lucky to meet someone like her? I wonder. A real friend. I wish I could see what she sees in me though. I feel like Kate would walk through fire for me—as I would for her. We're so much more than casual friends —even best friends. We protect each other like family would. The only problem is that I can't seem to protect Kate from the one person who hurts her the most—me. I'll admit it, I'm the one who causes the most pain and grief in her life. It's so obvious. All this emotional headfuckery I keep dragging her through. And even though I know all this and genuinely can't stand to see Kate in pain, I just can't stop myself from doing it…

Warm tears begin to rim the corners of my eyes. Containing myself, I quickly turn away, back towards the movie, before Kate can notice. Unaware of my tears, Kate's body slowly teeters closer, her head eventually coming to rest on my left shoulder. Without looking, I meekly slide my hand into hers.

"I just want you to know…" Kate begins to say, head still resting on my shoulder, "you'll never have to go through this alone. I'll always be here for you."

She sounds so earnest that my heart aches. I feel my thoughts start to sink once again, pulling me down inside myself like a sock puppet. I close my eyes and concentrate, lecturing myself to stay ever present.

Relax. Just breathe. In…out…in…out. Nice and slow. That's

right, everything's gonna be just fine. You're safe here. Kate's safe here. You have a sturdy roof over your head, good food, and each other's company. That's all you need. Remember, you are not alone. You are not alone...

Little by little, I feel my body start to relax—joints loosen, synapses dim. When Kate leaves my shoulder to take a drink, I scoot myself down on the bed until my head is resting on the pillow. Within seconds, I can feel my eyes start to get heavy. As is tradition, I'm always the first one to fall asleep during movie night. I can't help it. Sleepily, I glance back over at the movie one last time to see Frodo being warned of the many dangers that lie ahead.

As my eyes start to drift shut again, I picture the same scenario for Josh and Kate. They stand together at the mouth of an angry looking forest lined with twisted black. Before entering the tangled darkness, an ominous voice issues them a dire warning. The voice doesn't warn them about the demonic forest or magical entities. No, the only danger is my various flaws and mental inadequacies. What should be my burden alone to carry will soon be theirs as well. An emotional parasite that will feed off their natural happiness. Draining them. With this dark omen still ringing between my ears, I let out a bitter sigh and gently fall asleep.

The annoying buzz of my alarm is what wakes me the next morning. This in itself is pretty weird; I never set my alarm clock. Like, ever. I don't want that to be the first thing I hear every morning. It didn't take much thought for me to deduce that this must be Kate's doing. Yawning, I pry my tired eyes open and flop my hand around on the bedside table for my cellphone. 8 a.m. As I let out an aggravated sigh, silence the alarm, and set my phone down, I notice a letter resting on the bedside table. Rubbing my eyes, I reach out for the letter and read:

Good morning, beautiful,

Sorry to jet on you like this, but I decided to pick up a last-minute shift at the nursery. Please don't take me leaving so soon the wrong way. You know I need the overtime. Also, I took it upon myself to make you a suggested to-do list for the day. Nothing too excruciating, I swear. ;)

1. *Shower*
2. *Open curtains*
3. *Clean up a little*
4. *EAT AN ACTUAL MEAL!!!*

Remember, I'll be back over after my shift to check in on you. Be safe.

Love, Kate

Although I literally just woke up, I already feel like I don't possess the energy needed to accomplish anything on this list, including Kate coming back over after her shift. Right away, the idea frustrates me. The alarm, the list, the checkup—all of it. The whole shebang. This isn't even close to how I wanted to spend my day. Normally, I like to wake up whenever my body pleases. Why force it if I don't have to? Most of all, I just want to be left alone. I understand Kate just wants to help and steer me in the right direction, but this all feels very condescending. No, intrusive. Controlling, even.

But, hey, what do I know? It's only *MY* life.

DEAD ZONE
CHAPTER 8

The last week or so has gone by in a total blur. Honestly, I've spent most of it tucked away in bed. Ignoring anyone and everyone—including Josh. He's both texted and called me multiple times already. I even heard someone knock at the front door a few times. I'm assuming that was Josh too. Ugh, why can't he just take the hint already? Isn't it painfully obvious that I don't want anyone around me right now? What do I have to do to make him see that he deserves so much more than what I have to offer? I mean, seriously. When I first told him about my bipolar, he didn't even flinch. In fact, he went and researched the topic on his own time, teaching me some things that even I didn't know. I guess I'm grateful for his presence in my life, but I can't bear the thought of dragging another person down into the muck. I just can't.

Despite this anti-social streak of mine, Kate's been coming over every day to check in on me. Typical Kate, I know. When she stopped by this morning, she had a package. Well, actually, it was a brown paper bag. When I asked Kate what was in the bag, she said she didn't know, only that it was from Josh. I told her to leave the bag on the couch and haven't even looked at it since. I don't even want to think about it.

Still lounging in bed, I look over at the calendar Kate hung up on my bedroom wall. When I crash really hard like this, I lose all track of time. The days, hours, and minutes just melt together, forming one endless daydream of waking and sleeping. Conscious/unconscious. I suppose the calendar is Kate's way of helping me stay tethered to the present. Nice thought, but not exactly practical.

Not for me anyway.

I've had the urge to pee for the past three hours now. I keep telling myself that I should just get up and go to the bathroom already, but when I consider the long process, it makes me profoundly discouraged.

Step 1: Get out of bed.

Step 2: Walk to the bathroom.

Step 3: Open the door.

Step 4: Walk to the toilet.

Step 5: Pull down pants.

Step 6: Sit down.

Step 7: Pee.

Step 8: Toilet paper.

Step 9: Wipe.

Step 10: Stand up.

Step 11: Flush.

Step 12: Leave bathroom.

Step 13: Go back to bed.

All that just to empty my bladder. Not just a chore, but an ordeal. The way I figure, I'd be better off just not drinking at all. Well, maybe a couple sips of water every few hours or so. Would that be enough to sustain me? Needing a distraction, I look over to the crumpled paper bag on the couch.

Okay, I'll go pee, I tell myself, *and, on my way back to bed, I'll look at what's in the bag. It's silly to keep avoiding it. I gotta psych myself up and just do it. Okay…here we go…*

With too much exertion, I shove myself out of bed and shuffle my bloodless legs toward the bathroom. Once I go pee, I briefly consider giving up on my mission and just camping out on the toilet for the night. Knowing I can't do that, I sigh and force myself to keep going. Step by step. I have to see this through.

Once back in the warm cocoon of my bed, I realize that I forgot to grab the paper bag from the couch.

Shit, now I gotta get back up again. I'm such a dumbass. I hate breaking the blanket seal once I got it locked in.

Against my will, I get back up and retrieve the paper bag. Back in bed, I take a moment to admire the bag, noticing how neatly folded the top flap is.

What's in here? Hm, maybe it's a gift. Given the circumstances between Josh and I, probably not though. More likely, it's just some stuff I left over at his apartment. Maybe it's a letter from Josh saying that he wants nothing to do with me and hates my guts. A clean break. That would be best for everyone, I think.

Careful not to rip it, I unfold the bag and dump it out onto the bed. Among the bags contents are a letter, a candle stick, a lighter, a small crystal, and a single Polaroid picture. I pick up the picture first, squinting to better see it. In the picture, Josh and I are seen holding up a small crystal, both of us swooning with laughter. Giant red mountains loom in the background of the photo like sleeping giants. Right away, I recognize this picture; it was taken on our first date in

Sedona.

Needless to say, this wasn't at all what I was expecting. I expected the bag to contain one of my used toothbrushes, a scrunchy, or maybe an old bra and some shorts. Not this. Next is a letter written on folded notebook paper. Knowing this to be the moment of truth, I unfold the letter and read:

Dear Sarah,

I know you're deep in your own head right now. I get it. Well, not really, but you know what I mean. And as much as I wish I could be there to help walk you back through that inner maze, I know you want your privacy. And that's okay. I hope it's not overstepping, but I asked Kate to deliver this bag to you. I did this in the hopes that you might use the enclosed items to help keep yourself in the Grounded. I think the picture of us in Sedona captured a magical moment in time. I know you probably still remember that day. There were those new age crystal shops on every corner, each one packed with shiny stones that supposedly cure all physical and mental ailments. I remember watching you grab some random crystal and close your eyes.

Seconds later, you opened your eyes again and announced, "I can now confirm that this crystal does not cure bipolar."

This is how you told me that you had bipolar. You watched to see what my reaction would be. Do you remember what I said back? I picked up the same crystal, squeezed my eyes closed, waited a few seconds, then opened them again and said, "I can confirm that this crystal is useless but looks very cool."

Enclosed is that same crystal. Please use it as a reminder that bipolar is something you <u>have</u>, not something that you <u>are</u>. You are Sarah. You are a beautiful, brilliantly talented human being. You are worth being loved. You are not a burden. You are not worthless. Please *don't take this the wrong way, but you're a lot like Frodo from Lord of the Rings. Like you, Frodo is forced to set out on a long, arduous adventure and eventually emerges triumphant. Despite the odds, he pushed through the worst set of obstacles imaginable. Just like I know you will.*

Finally, the candle and lighter. These items are pretty straight forward. I'm sure you've been lying in the dark for weeks now. Sometimes, the smallest bit of light is all we need to find our way through dark times. I love you, Sarah. With all my heart, I do. Please, remember that Kate and I are waiting for you on the other side of the maze. We will give you all the tools we can to help bring you back. Regardless of how you may feel now, I know the real you is still in there somewhere. Try to hold on and know that I'll be here. Waiting.

Love, Josh

I shove the letter under my pillow and lay back down. I realize that there are really two versions of myself—two separate Sarah's living inside of one body. There's the Sarah that runs my heart and the Sarah that runs my head. These two versions of myself represent both who I want to be, and the seething monster that I'm afraid of turning into. No matter how much a try to avoid it, it always finds me in the end. It lurks through the shadows of my mind, waiting for just the right moment to jump out and show its ugly face.

Sullenly, I place the candle on my bedstand and light its sharp, white wick. A small flame flourishes, eating away at the blanket of darkness that hangs over the room. I lay back down and simply watch the candle, admiring its wisp of dancing yellow light. As I continue to stare, I can feel my eyes begin to burn. Regardless of the growing discomfort, I keep staring at the tiny flame. Unblinking. I scrupulously watch as the flame dances and sways on its raised platform, every small movement captured on the darkened walls around me. After about ten minutes of watching, I see a fat bead of melted wax break away from the top of the candle and roll down the side. I watch as the bead slows to a stop and hardens just before reaching the table.

You know…I'm just like this candle. Burning bright while slowly cannibalizing myself. Helpless to watch as huge pieces of myself just melt away. Gone forever. Forming a hardened puddle of who I once was. This candle will eventually be unrecognizable, burned down to nothing, just as I will be. I can feel it happening. Any day now, the darkness will finally take over and put an end to all this. To me…

Bead by bead, I watch the candle shrink. Smaller and smaller. Burning all the way down to just a lumpy puddle of discolored wax, the flame now struggles to stay alive. It grows dimmer, barely able to keep its head above waxy water. Then, in one last subtle hiss, the flame is gone— leaving only a tail of extinguished smoke in its wake.

Just then, I hear my apartment door slowly creak open.

"Sarah?!" Kate yells into the dank darkness of my apartment. "Sarah, you still here?!"

"What?!" I yell back.

Kate immediately walks over to the nearest window and flings open the curtains. The bright light feels like a million tiny knives stabbing my eyes. Shielding my face from the attack, I peek through my fingers at the clock on the wall. Apparently, I had just spent twelve consecutive hours staring at a burning candle.

"Ooph, when's the last time you took a shower?" Kate asks. "Stinks in here." She didn't wait for an answer before yanking the blankets off my bed and throwing them to the floor. Initially, I say nothing in return; I know this is just rhetorical question. She knows damn well I haven't taken a shower since the last time I was forced to.

"Look, I'll make you a deal," Kate starts to say. "If you get up, take a shower, and spend the day with me… I promise that I'll leave you alone all day tomorrow. What'd you say, hm?"

It's useless; she'll never take no for an answer. This little game of 21 Questions is only the beginning. Kate won't stop until I cave. Asking for my compliance is only her way of making me feel like I have a choice.

"Fine…whatever…" I drag myself out of bed and head towards the bathroom. After I take a hot shower, I grab a clean towel and wrap it around my body. Standing before the full-length mirror hanging on the back of the bathroom door, I wipe the film of fog away and take a good, long look at myself. In an instant, I'm reminded of the night I met Josh. More specifically, I remember staring at myself in a mirror while waiting in line to use the bathroom. Looking at my reflection then, I felt like I was under an intoxicating spell. I was not only optimistic and confident, but powerful. Now, when I look at myself, all I see is an empty shell. A human shaped void. The person staring back isn't me that I know. Not really. The real me is still trying to find her way out of the lightless maze.

I try to reach out mentally to this lost, inner version of myself, but I get no response. Where is she? How far in has she gotten? My heart weeps when I think about how sad and alone she must feel in there. I know she's trying desperately to find her way back to the light.

Outwardly, I whisper, "I'm so sorry."

After getting dressed, I walk out of the bathroom and again come face to face with Kate. Always chipper, she smiles warmly at me and asks, "Ready?"

Reluctantly, I roll my eyes and nod.

As if I were cattle, Kate herds me over to the front door and swings it wide open—motioning for me to step out first. I try to stall, defiantly crossing my arms over my chest, and nervously ask, "Where are we even going?"

"We're going on an adventure! Come on, let's get going already."

Kate and I left the apartment and headed downstairs to her car. Once there, Kate excitedly ushered me into the passenger seat before climbing in behind the wheel. "Buckle up, please," she says as she checks her mirror and pulls us out onto the roadway.

As we ride through light downtown traffic, I only have enough energy to moodily sit and stare out my side window. I hope this will be enough to tell Kate that I'm not in the mood for small talk. But, not even five minutes into the drive, she turns to me and excitedly says, "So, we got two stops to make today. I think you'll be happy to know that the first stop is for coffee!"

Kate knows that I love a good iced coffee. I mean, who doesn't? My favorite drink isn't anything fancy, mostly caramel flavored milk with an added splash of dark coffee. Even so, I do miss my daily iced coffee. I almost forgot how much joy they bring me every time I have one.

Within minutes, I see the coffee shop slide into view outside my window. As Kate and I both step out of the car and approach the shop, I hear someone inside yell my name as soon as we open the door.

"Sarah!" Stephanie, a barista, cheers. "I was wondering when you'd be back! You want the usual? Iced caramel latte, right?"

Although I don't want to, I can't help but smile at her warmness. "Yes, please. And Kate will take a cup of whatever nasty stuff she usually gets. Thank you."

Stephanie chuckles from behind the service counter. "Ah, okay. So, a regular cup of black coffee for Kate then? Comin' right up."

Kate smiles. "Thanks, Steph."

We then move over to a table for two and have a seat and wait. Within seconds, I can feel myself starting to zone out, my fingers weirdly fiddling with each other while resting in my lap. Suddenly, I hear Kate tap one hard knuckle on the tabletop to get my attention.

"Hi there," she says when I finally look up and make eye contact.

"Oh...hi."

I can feel my heart begin to soften. How could anyone not love this woman? As we continue to lock eyes, I feel the hot sting of fresh tears start to surface. I try my best to stand against the incoming tide of emotions, but the current is strong.

Stop it! a part of me inwardly chastises. *Can't you see that Kate's just trying to help?! She's only doing what she feels is right for you. Christ, at least somebody cares about your well-being. Can everyone say that? No, I don't think so. Kate knows better than anybody that if you get stuck in this rut for too long…well…it'll end badly…*

Stephanie walks up to our table and hands us our coffees. "Enjoy, ladies." Before walking away, she turns back and adds, "Oh, and Sarah, this is for you too." Stephanie then hands me a rectangular box.

With an exaggerated gasp, Kate croons, "Whoa! What'd we have here?! A mystery box?! How exciting! I wonder what's inside!"

I roll my eyes. "Hmm, I wonder. Whatever could this be?"

Right away, I can tell the box belonged to Kate because it's for a pair of size 8 Teva brand sandals. When I jokingly scan the side of the box and then promptly look under the table at Kate's feet, she sheepishly tries to hide them.

Eyes wide and smiling bright, Kate urges, "Just open it!"

I open the box and peek inside. Inside is a gold ring, a DVD of *The Lord of the Rings*, a bag of Cheetos, a coke, and a letter. When I look back across the table at Kate, she's on the verge of tears. Instead of crying, she pushes the feelings down and clears her tightened throat. She knows all these things are my comfort items for when I am depressed.

"Ready for stop number two?" she asks.

I nod, grab the letter, and shove it into my purse to read later. Grabbing the box and my coffee, Kate and I stand up and head for the door.

"Bye, ladies! Enjoy your day!" Stephanie calls from behind the counter. In unison, Kate and I both walk and wave to her through the glass storefront.

As we're walking back to the car, Kate suddenly stops in her tracks, spins around and wraps me up in a big hug. My heart nearly breaks. Normally, Kate doesn't show this much emotion when I'm struggling. I think she is afraid it will make things worse for me. This is the second time in the last few weeks that she has gotten this emotional. I know she must be worried. Not knowing any other way to react, I hug her back. Like being exposed to intense gamma radiation, I can feel her love filtering through every layer of my being. Although it's hard, I have to try and snap back out of this. If not for myself, then for Kate.

Still hugging me tight, she whispers, "I love you, Sarah."

"I love you too, Kate," I whisper back.

When Kate finally let's go, she quickly wipes her leaky eyes and smiles. "You ready for an adventure?"

I match her smile and say, "You know it, baby."

"Alright, then we're off to Mordor!"

To this, I tilt my head back and laugh. "Stop! You're such a nerd—"

A split second later, I get the grave sense that something's wrong. The joyous laughter is instantly replaced with a deep spike of mortal dread. Suddenly, a large, metallic shape becomes caught in my peripherals. Although it's blurred, I see it coming in fast at Kate's backside. I open my mouth to scream, to warn Kate that she's standing in the direct line of danger, but nothing comes out. My voice just isn't there. Then, in the span of ceaseless moments, everything goes black.

That's the last thing I remember.

THE CRASH
CHAPTER 9

I'm awake but unable to open my eyes.

All I can do is lay here in this bed and listen. Nothing else. I can't move, see or speak. Dazed, it feels like my skull is packed tight with tiny balls of cotton. This makes it hard for me to decipher between what's real and imaginary. Every time I try to concentrate through the fog and open my eyes, invisible fingers seem to clamp them down from the other side.

Sometimes I can hear people talking, but their voices are extremely muffled—distant conversations caught on the traveling wind. Unable to do literally anything but listen, I put all my focus on those voices. Every last ounce. Eventually, after what felt like years of studying the wind, the voices became clearer. There's a male and female voice, and they're talking about me. The male voice seems familiar somehow, but I can't quite place it. Then, like a freight train, the realization hits me—it's Josh.

"Have you let your parents know yet?" I hear the woman ask.

"Parents are dead," Josh flatly says. "I'm all she has left."

What's he talking about? Where am I? What the fuck's going on here?

I have to open my mouth and say something, but when I

try, nothing happens. My lips are shut. Paralyzed, I feel like a prisoner trapped in my own busted body.

"Well, you're a wonderful brother," the female voice says. "I'm sure Sarah's going to be very grateful to see you once she wakes up."

There's a slight pause before Josh clears his throat and awkwardly asks, "When do you think that'll be?"

"When she's ready," the woman evenly responds.

With great effort, I manage to pry my eye lids open just a crack. This in itself is exhausting. Defeated, I have no choice but to let my heavy eyelids slam shut again after only a few seconds. Once again, I was trapped.

Why's Josh pretending to be my brother? I'm so confused. Where am I right now? Where's Kate? Oh God…I hope she's okay—

My inner woes are interrupted when I hear Josh's voice, loud and clear, ask, "Sarah? Sarah, can you hear me?" He's at my bedside now. I can feel his presence.

I try again to move, to reach out to him, but am still much too weak. I feel my right index finger move a little bit at the command, but that's it. Everything feels so heavy, as if my bones were encased in steel. Slowly, I manage to crack my eyelids open again. Somehow, I dig deep, holding them open a little longer this time. Problem is, my vision is totally shot. There's no definition to my surroundings, the room made up of amorphous blobs of color. Feeling disoriented by all the fuzzy lights and shapes, I allow my eyes to drift shut again.

"Looks like she might be waking up soon," I hear the woman say. "I'll give you guys some privacy." I listen as her padded footsteps disappear down a distant hallway.

Where's Kate? Why isn't she here? I mean, I appreciate Josh being here, but I'd much rather see Kate right now. I need to see her. I think I'll just keep my eyes closed until Kate gets here. Not sure if I can handle being alone with Josh…especially like this…

When I try to voice these concerns, my mouth still won't move. The scent of Josh's cologne wafts past my nose. I can literally feel how anxious he is. Beyond worried. I start to concentrate on opening my eyes all the way. Success. I can keep them open. Soon, I'm able to unseal my lips too. Although I'm fully awake inside my head, my body continues to put up a fight. But I refuse to let it win. Not this time.

"Sarah, I'm right here," Josh says, cupping my hand in his.

It takes a good minute or so for my vision to clear, but when it does, I immediately recognize where I am. A hospital room. Remaining still to conserve my energy, I continue to scan my surroundings. Josh is sitting directly to my left. I look over to my right and see a tall machine. Its many wires and tubes are plugged into various points on my body, feeding and draining from me.

Weakly, I turn my head to the side to face Josh. His face is fully flushed, paler than a glass of whole milk. He looks like he hasn't slept in days—eyes red and puffy. As I slowly look away, realigning my sight back to the ceiling, I take a moment to concentrate on wiggling my toes. It wasn't easy, but I did it. Finally, some real progress.

Oh, thank God, I'm not paralyzed. Warm tears of gratitude start to trickle down my cheeks.

"Hey," Josh says softly, gently placing one hand on my shoulder.

I look over at him, observing his body language. His smile is there, but very uneasy, as if he is hiding some horrible truth. This expression scares me. I watch as Josh reaches forward to gently wipe away the trail of tears from my face. Something bad has happened. I can feel it. I try frantically to remember what happened before I woke up in this bed but can't.

Then, the dam broke; all the memories came flooding back.

"I'm so sorry, Sarah," Josh solemnly says while lightly squeezing my hand.

No…no this can't be real, I tell myself. *This can't really be happening…*

My heart's racing a million miles a minute. I try to process all this new information but there's no use. It's all way too much. Needing to get up and find Kate, I claw at the edge of the bed, trying to prop myself up into a sitting position. I don't know where I'll go, but I don't care; I just need to find her. Unfortunately, my legs refuse to work. When I try to move them, they just sit there like two pale salami sticks. Unmoving. In a crackly whisper, I turn to Josh and beg, "Please…help me."

As I begin attempting to yank out the many tubes in my arms, Josh jumps up from his chair and pleads, "Hey, stop that! Don't try to get up! Just lay back and calm down!"

I ignore him; I need to know what's going on. I need to find Kate. I need to be there for Kate when she wakes up. She shouldn't have to do this alone. I calm myself down enough to get a single quiet sentence out to Josh.

"Where…is…she?" I gasp, mouth dryer than a sand bucket.

Nervously, Josh rubs at the back of his neck.

"She's…ugh…there was an accident…" My mind goes numb. An accident? How bad of an accident? Before I can push him any further on the matter, Josh breaks down in a fit of tears. I don't need to hear any more. Terrified, I wait for him to stop sobbing and look back up at me again.

"Sarah, I'm so sorry, but both you and Kate were struck by a drunk driver. Your injuries were all minor…but Kate…Kate didn't make it. She's dead."

I close my eyes and attempt to absorb those final words. Kate's dead. I feel like I now have only two choices: I can either kill myself or kill the asshole that did this to us. No in-betweens. What would Kate think of these choices? Pretty sure she wouldn't approve of either one. Revenge or not, I'm dangerously close to breaking. I know the result is inevitable, but—please not here. Not now.

Needing to talk about literally anything else, I crane my head back over to Josh and ask, "Why are you telling people that you're my brother?"

I can see Josh is thrown off by this question. I'm sure he expected something else entirely after the massive bombshell he just dropped on me.

"W-well," he stutters, stifling back tears, "I think Kate must've listed me as one of her emergency contacts. When I got the call about Kate, I knew you were involved somehow. As for the brother thing…well…I knew if I said I was your brother the nurses wouldn't restrict my visitation. I needed to know if you were okay."

That makes me wonder, *Who's my emergency contact again? Oh yeah…it's Kate…*

"I want to go home," I hear myself say. Nerves

unraveling, I feel myself becoming fully detached from the situation. Physically and mentally separated. Like a self-mechanized being, programmed for only the simplest autonomous actions.

Just then, a nurse enters the room and approaches my bedside.

"Hi, Sarah. I'm Nurse Renae. I've been helping to look after you for the past few days."

"Huh?" I gasp. "Did you say *days*?! Really?! I've been out for days?!"

"Well, technically, you woke up a day after the accident," Josh explains, "but the nurses had to sedate you because you wouldn't stop screaming for Kate. I was here for some of it. You almost clocked a few of the doctors on duty. They finally decided to sedate you after you tried ripping the IVs out."

The nurse speaks up to add, "You just weren't ready to wake up yet, dear. That's all."

Tongue just a leathery flap of sandpaper, I look to the nurse and ask, "When can I go home?"

Nurse Renae references the chart hanging at the end of the bed, flipping through its many pages, before saying, "Looks like you'll be approved for release later today. Just need to find someone to sign you out and give you a ride home. Also, some one-on-one care at home for the next forty-eight hours or so would be ideal as well. If you want those broken ribs to heal properly, you'll have to take it easy. Having someone around to lend a helping hand is never a bad thing."

Josh roughly clears his throat. "Uhm…I'm actually her

ride. Is there paperwork I need to fill out or do I just—"

Drowning out all outside conversation, I close my eyes. *I can't believe it…Kate's dead. What do I do now? More importantly…how will I do it without her?*

As Josh pulls the car up to the front of my apartment building, I feel my bones shake with cold trepidation. Hazily, I stare out my side window at the tall apartment building. Still slightly high from the medication, I zone out on the endless lattice of mossy bricks as Josh rounds the car and opens my passenger side door.

"Stop," I groggily snap, blinking the lattice away, "I can open my own door. Thanks."

Better watch out; the last person to open the door for me is dead now.

Josh says nothing, only steps back so I can swoon my way out onto the sidewalk. Step by step, I trudge my way up to my apartment. Josh makes sure to follow close behind, eyes carefully watching but lips sealed. He knows I'm in a very sensitive space right now. One false move and…

After unlocking my apartment door, I take two steps inside and then just stand there. Facing forward, looking in at my lonely apartment. I don't know why I do this. Eventually, I continue moving down the long hallway and cut the corner to my bed. I envision Kate running to that same bed to execute one of her famous bellyflops. The memories make me both smile and cry. When Josh notices my knees become visibly weak, he jumps forward to help me keep sturdy. But I am quick to shrug him off and keep moving forward.

As I move, I glance over at the coffee table by the couch and see flowers and cards. I can tell by the handwriting on the cards that they're probably from Mags. I'm sure the flowers are from Sam and Sylvia. I wonder how they're handling all this. I'm sure they've tried texting or calling me by now, but I don't care. To be honest, I'll probably never talk to them again. Without Kate, what would be the point?

Once I reach the bed, I climb under the covers and turn onto my side. There, the melted puddle of wax on my nightstand remains. Cold and hard. I hear Josh set some bags on the counter in the kitchen before slowly making his way back to the bedroom.

"I want to be alone now," I say, eyes never leaving the dark puddle of wax.

"But the nurse said someone should be here to help you with—"

Curtly, I turn to him and raise my voice. "Josh…I said…I WANT TO BE ALONE."

The room grows deathly quiet. I can practically hear his thoughts:

"Well, Sarah, I'm sorry, but you don't have much of a choice. I can't just leave you here. That would be irresponsible. What if you hurt yourself?"

Although a part of me feels sad for him, I feel sadder for myself. No one will ever love me the way Kate did. Nobody. Not now, not ever again. Kate was my rock, my one beacon of light in this impossibly dark world. And now…there's only darkness.

"One more thing," Josh starts to say as he watches me climb into bed. "I'm not sure what you want me to do with this. They told me it was recovered from the accident. Thought you might like to keep it." In Josh's hands is the box that Kate gave me. The box meant for stop number two—the stop we never got to make. Just then, I remember the letter Kate gave me that day. I think I last had it in my purse.

"Where's my purse?!" I ask, voice streaked with intense desperation.

Josh leaps into action and grabs my purse from the couch and hands it to me. Without hesitation, I dump everything out onto the bed. There it is: the letter from Kate. She knew I couldn't read it in front of her. I grab the letter and squeeze it to my chest. This is the last thing that Kate will ever communicate to me. I open my tear-stained eyes and look over at Josh. I see he's also crying.

"If you want me to leave, I'll leave. Just please try and stay safe. I'll text every few hours to check in…if that's okay with you, that is."

I nod. Although I don't say it, I have no intention of responding to any of his texts. I've never wanted to be alone so badly in my entire life.

Josh walks over and gently kisses the top of my head, letting his warm lips linger. As he turns and heads for the door, I watch him stop halfway. "I'm here for you, Sarah. Whenever you're ready…I'll be here."

He doesn't wait for a response. I hear the front door open, then creak shut again. Finaly alone, I focus on the letter. A pitter-patter of tears stains the plain white paper as I hold it. I try to wipe them away before they can damage the ink. This letter must be preserved. With trembling fingers, I read:

"*Dear*   *Sarah…*"

AUTOPILOT
CHAPTER 10

Dreams have always fascinated me. Are dreams my subconscious teaching me something?

Last night I had a nightmare. I was running through a forest while the rain poured down on me. The sky was full of dark clouds. Far in the distance I could see a little girl running away from me. She was wearing a white nightgown and no shoes. Her brown hair flowing behind her. I called out to her, "Hey! Please stop!" but she continued to run. Was she running from me? Could she hear me? Who was she?

Off in the distance is a small shack. The girl ran up to it and through the front door, slamming it shut behind her. I finally made it to the front door of the shack. Out of breath, I walked up to the door and knock. While waiting, I looked around the area from the porch. There were no roads leading to this shack. I didn't hear any noise coming from inside. I turned the knob and slowly pushed the door open.

The inside of the cabin was dark. The only visible light was coming through a boarded-up broken window and the light from the open door behind me. I stood in the doorway for a moment allowing my eyes to adjust. There appeared to be just one large room. Like a studio. I squinted my eyes and saw a chair in the middle of the room, like a chair used in a hair salon. The little girl was sitting there with her back toward me.

"Hello, are you OK?" I asked.

She didn't respond. She didn't move.

Cautiously, I walked up to the chair. Once I reached it, I slowly turned it around to have her face me. I jumped back at what I saw. Her mouth was wide open, completely black inside. A dark hole. Her eyes were the same as her mouth. Nothingness. I was frozen there in front of her. Unable to scream or run even though I was begging myself to.

When I woke up, my bed sheets were soaked in sweat. Heart still racing from the prophetic dream, I looked around the darkened bedroom, allowing my eyes time to adjust just like I had in the dream. I recently put black curtains up over the windows. I find a small amount of solace in them, as they block out all distractions from the outside world. The clock on the wall read three, but I'm not sure if it's a.m. or p.m.

I crawl out of bed and crack the curtains just enough to see outside. Still dark. Must be morning.

Thinking about Josh, I crawl back into bed. I know the relationship we once had is now long over. It was inevitable; I could only keep up this charade for so long. I don't even know what's real anymore. My brain is constantly deceiving me. I wonder just how long this phase will last. I haven't pulled myself out of a deep depression like this without Kate's help in over ten years. She was my anchor. Without her, there's no telling where the sea of life will pull me.

Will this be the one that kills me?

Living with bipolar is a lot like being a hamster on a wheel. You just run and run, never really going anywhere. The only thing that ever changes is what's inside your head.

Your mindset drastically changes day by day, minute by minute, second by second. Good or bad, you never know when or how your mood might change. These changes are unrelenting and, most of all, dangerous. This goes for anyone unlucky enough to cross my path as well.

I'm in this battle for the rest of my life. It's not fair; I do enjoy being around people. I want to enjoy life to the fullest just like anyone else would. I want so badly to be the person that people see me as. I don't want to constantly be fighting in my own head, masking the whole thing with a flimsy smile. I'm both Dr. Jekyll and Mr. Hyde. But I must have sovereignty over my own body and mind. Too bad I'll be forever judged for these faults, faults I never asked for in the first place. Cruel fate or not, I must live with the consequences of having this feral mind. This disease makes me feel like I'm nothing more than an empty vessel—an unwilling host to the growing sickness inside. I just want to disappear off the face of the earth.

Would probably be better for everybody if I did.

I haven't heard from Josh in two days. He came by the apartment to ask me if I needed a ride to Kate's funeral later that same day. I said no. That's probably the moment when he came to realize just how much of a piece of shit I really am. I know it was disrespectful not to attend, but I just couldn't go through with it. I needed my best friend there for moral support. At my side, not laying in an open casket.

When I wouldn't answer Josh's calls on the day of Kate's funeral, he just showed up at my doorstep. At first, I refused to answer the door. He then stood out there for over an hour and yelled to me through the door, begging me not to miss the funeral.

"C'mon, Sarah!" he said. "I know this is hard, but we need to pay our respects! Think of how Kate's family will feel if her best friend doesn't show up! Please, do the right thing!"

But I ignored him. Finally, Josh left for the funeral without me. Once I was sure he was gone, I opened the front door and saw a folded-up pamphlet wedged into the crease of the outer doorframe. Quickly, I snatched up the paper and went back inside. At first, I couldn't bring myself to open it. I didn't need a silly color pamphlet to tell me what I already knew about Kate. The only thing I didn't know was where Kate would be buried. Heading back to the bedroom, I tossed the pamphlet into the top drawer of my nightstand before the urge to look at it became too great to ignore.

Josh is wrong, I told myself as I eased my tired body back into bed. *I doubt Kate's family will be devastated by my absence. They knew better than anybody how my bipolar affected Kate. They hated how I reminded Kate of her brother, Trevor. I guarantee they didn't hate it as much as I did though.*

As I lay in bed, I turn over and see the letter that Kate wrote sitting on the bedside table. It's wadded up into a ball now. I could only read the first line or so before completely losing my shit. I haven't looked at it since. I lay there for a few hours drifting in and out of sleep. I dream about the letter and what it says. I wake up finally when I swear, I can hear her voice calling out to me from the page. I try to look away from the discarded letter but can't. Needing to know, I reach across the bed, grab the letter, and smooth out the ball in my lap. Eyes cutting through the gloom, I start from the beginning:

Dear Sarah,

Well…we're here! I know we've been here before and will probably be here again. Although bipolar may be incurable, that doesn't mean you have to suffer alone. I know you're deep in your head right now, you know I can always tell. Just remember, you are not alone. You must fight against these voices, allow the good to triumph over evil. So, with that theme in mind, our second stop of the day will be a Lord of the Rings movie marathon! This is nonnegotiable, by the way. We're going to eat junk food and watch Frodo fight the temptation of the ring, just like you do with your bipolar.

I love you, Sarah! Always will. You're my bestest friend in the whole wide world. Never forget that.

> *-Kate*

As I let the letter fall from my hands, a sudden burst of anger plumes up inside of me.

What…the fuck? WHAT THE FUCK?! Fight the temptation? Are you fucking serious? You think this is a fucking choice? You think this is a temptation that can be avoided?

Outwardly, I scream, "This isn't a fucking choice, Kate!"

Much too angry to remain in bed, I jump up and pace in circles around the bedroom.

How many people actually think this is a choice for me? Do they really think I'm choosing this fucked-up life for myself? Maybe they don't think I try hard enough, is that it? How could they possibly understand the internal battle I fight every single day. No one. They don't understand what it's like to be this screwed up, always self-

sabotaging and burning myself. I can't even trust my own senses.

Suddenly, a thought occurs: *Wait...does Josh feel this way about me too?*

Riding that foaming swell of adrenaline, I march back over to the nightstand and grab my phone. I scroll through my contacts until coming across Josh's number. Somewhere deep inside, a small voice begs me not to make the call. They know this won't end well. Ignoring that tiny voice of reason, I hit the call button and brace myself for impact. I listen as the phone rings and rings, but no one answers. Eventually, the call goes to voicemail, and I hang up without leaving a message.

Why did I ever think anyone could love me? People like me aren't capable of being loved. We were a misprint on the paper. We are the words with no autocorrect suggestions— Suddenly, my phone begins to ring. It's Josh.

I take a deep breath before accepting the call. "Hello?"

"Sarah, hey, I'm so sorry I didn't answer. Are you okay? What's wrong?" He sounds tired, as if half asleep.

"Oh, I'm sorry, was I interrupting something?" I ask in a very condescending voice.

There is a long pause before Josh uneasily responds, "Sarah, it's 3:30 in the morning. I was sleeping."

I ignore his excuse to bluntly ask, "Do you think this is a choice for me? Don't bullshit me."

"Huh? A choice? A choice for what? What're you talking about?"

"My fucking bipolar, Josh!" I erupt. "Do you think I want this?! Do you think I want to lose everyone I've ever loved?! Do you think I choose to be miserable and alone?! Well, do you?!" As I start to break down and cry, Josh remains silent. "I'm alone, Josh. And I'll always be alone." Through a veil of tears, I ignore the awkwardness of the conversation and push forward. "I die a little bit every time this happens, you know. Every time I lose somebody. I don't want this. Any of it. I just want to be normal. I can't tell what's real anymore." Pausing to catch my breath, I add, "Did you mean it when you said you loved me? Or was that just bullshit too?"

"Sarah, I do love you," Josh patiently counters. "Please, let me come over to help you. I just want to help."

Although a long pause falls over the call, my brain is teeming with tormented thoughts. "You can't love me, Josh," I mumble numbly, barely aware of my own body. "No one can love me."

Before Josh could respond, I end the call and shut off my phone. The noise in my head is getting louder. Fiercer. Needing escape, I frantically open the nightstand drawer and start digging through it. There should be papers with information on bipolar in here somewhere. Kate researched it for me a little while back. But when I find the papers resting at the very bottom of the drawer, I can't bring myself to concentrate on the words. Frustrated, I chuck the papers across the room and watch them scatter.

Head screaming, I lower myself to the floor and cross my legs—fingers pushing into my ears so hard that it feels like I might puncture straight into my brain. I need silence. I need peace of mind.

"Please help me, please help me," I whisper. To whom? I don't know. I close my eyes and become instantly lost in my thoughts. Of course, my thoughts gravitate towards Kate.

I tried. I really did. I tried to catch the triggers, but I still fell. Headfirst too. I know this isn't what you would've wanted for me, Kate. I know I should stay present, but I can't stop myself from falling. The pull is just too strong.

I feel like I'm dangling off the edge of a very high cliff. When I try to pull myself back up to safety, something from below keeps pulling me back down. Demonic voices urge me to let go. Succumb to the darkness. On the ledge above, the other version of me—the *real* me—holds out her hand.

"Please, help me…" I beg. "I…I can't hold on much longer."

The version of me on the ledge opens her mouth but doesn't say a word. Her expression is so sad, so drained. I know she doesn't want me to fall, but her body refuses to come any closer. Mirrored tears stream down our cheeks. My arms hurt; fingers splitting at the ends. As I consider my options, I hear a voice from below say, *'Don't worry, just let go. Stop fighting and give in to us. Just let go."*

All logic begins to fade. I look back up at the ledge, watching my alternate self slowly become transparent. As all the color slowly drains from her being, she looks down at me once more. Her mouth opens wide again, but still no sound. Although she's fading fast, there's immense desperation in those eyes. She knows what's to come next. As do I.

I can't hold on. I can't do this. What's the point? Why should I even hold on?

I take a deep breath inward and let go of the ledge. As I fall backward toward the dark abyss, the girl on the ledge watches me with tears in her eyes. I close my own eyes and completely disappear. Back to the darkness. Back to the bottom. Back to the beginning of the maze.

As if possessed, I see myself get out of bed and head to the bathroom. I think there's some Valium left in the medicine cabinet. And if there is, I intend to use it. As I open the cabinet door and fish out the bottle, the noise in my head becomes deafening. Pill bottle in hand, I waste no time twisting off the cap. I open my mouth wide and down the entire bottle. Using the sink, I then fill the empty bottle with some water to help wash them down.

Leaving the bathroom, I stumble my way over the couch. As I sit down, aching head cradled in my hands, I feel the inner noise gradually start to fade. Not all at once, but little by little. But as my head clears, my eyes start to lose focus, as if I were looking through a lens of chlorinated underwater. Next, my body starts to tingle all over. This is about the time that I realize that I've made a huge mistake. I briefly consider calling Josh for help but ultimately decide against it.

What's the point? I'm done dragging people into my shit. This ends now, it ends now...

I try to stand up from the couch but can't figure out how. My limbs feel like they've been dipped in quick-drying cement. Weighted. I feel fear trying to invade my mind, but something is suppressing it. I hate how much I'm enjoying this newfound silence. Unable to act, I feel my mannequin body start to slide off the couch and onto the floor.

Mind quiet—eyes heavy—I feel myself drifting off to the void.

Suddenly, a faint voice brings me back from the edge of sleep. I manage to prop my eyes open just long enough to see my body rise up off the floor. Effortlessly, as if lighter than a feather, I feel myself rise up through the ceiling and into the sky. I must be dreaming. When I close my eyes again, everything goes black. A few seconds later, I hear the voice again. This time, I immediately recognize it to be Kate's. When I open my eyes, I'm floating over the coffee shop. Even from my elevated angle, I can see Kate and I are standing by the street, just like we had done on the day of the accident. It all feels so real. I close my eyes and hear Kate whisper, "I love you, Sarah."

When I open my eyes again, I'm driving across a fog laden bridge. The fog is so thick that I can barely see two feet ahead. There're no other cars in sight. As I'm driving, I spot a lone woman standing on the outer ledge of the bridge, ready to jump. My mind now laser focused, I slam the car into park and jump out. I feel anxious as I approach the woman and begin to gently coax them not to jump.

"You don't want to do this," I plead. "You have so much left to live for. This is just a single hard moment; it too will pass."

I go on to say that she should consider how this will make her family and friends feel—the rift that will be created in her loss. I ask lots of questions to remind her that jumping isn't the answer to her problems. Finally, the woman turns away from the ledge and faces me. Tears stream down her face, cutting faint lines across her pale skin. I can literally feel her pain. Brown, curly hair pulled back into a low ponytail; her striking blue eyes seem to stare right through me. I can't quite place it, but something's so familiar about her.

"It's so loud," the woman whispers. "Too loud. Too often. I just can't take it anymore." When I reassure her that the noise will go away, the woman offers me a faint smile. "Why did you wait so long to come?"

A moment of panic. Somehow, I'm getting through to her but am now scared that I might mess it up and say the wrong thing. One wrong move could result in a tragic fatality. So, with great care, I keep my voice even and my body language lax.

"I was trying to find you," I say. "It took me a little longer than I expected. I'm here now though. Please, back away from the ledge." Slowly, I watch as the woman climbs down from the bridge's high railing and approaches me. Once we are facing each other, I whisper, "We can't keep meeting like this, you know."

She nods in agreement. "I know. We must try harder."

I smile, knowing that the cycle has now been reset. The ordeal might be over, but not forever. We will meet here again. And again. Until the end of all time. How do I know all this?

Well, because I am her and she is me.

DIAGNOSED
CHAPTER 11

I still remember when I first found out that I had bipolar. At the time, I was seeing a regular therapist three to four times a week. One on one. That was, until I got my diagnosis. After that, I started missing more and more appointments. A few at first, then a lot. I must've used every excuse in the book. Every fib from belly aches, false emergencies, and laundry. Then, one day, I just decided not to go back at all. I was convinced that I didn't need some shrink overanalyzing my every thought and feeling. What do they know anyway? No, I was determined to fix my problems all on my own. No therapy, no emotional crutches. I knew this would require extensive research, not to mention the ability to take an in-depth look at past childhood experiences and recall hidden patterns of trauma. It didn't take long for me to become obsessed with trying to cure my bipolar. I felt like one of those gritty private investigators from the 50s. Locked away for days in my dimly lit apartment—handwritten notes and reminders plastered all over the walls like clues to an unsolved murder. This was by far my biggest cold case, my great white whale of a mystery that was begging to be solved. I filled so many spiral notebooks with random theories and tidbits. I honestly can't even remember how many. Anything and everything to do with what was going on inside my head got written down. I even took the time to learn about all the available medications offered by both "Big Pharma" and lesser-known holistic gurus.

At a great risk to my personal well-being, I was wholly determined to leave no stone unturned. Whatever the cost.

One night, during this obsessive mania, I got a random text message from Kate. We weren't that close at this point in our friendship. More like casual acquaintances. But ever since that night she picked me up from the hospital, we would occasionally text each other. Never anything serious, just casual back-and-forth. But on this one particular late-night text exchange, things played out very differently.

Hey, Sarah. You busy right now?

Initially, I considered not responding. But, for some reason, I went against my anti-social urges and typed back: *Hey, Kate. I'm not busy, just doing some research. What's up?*

Not even two seconds after I hit send, Kate messaged back: *Cool if I come over? No big deal if you aren't up for it.*

I looked up from my phone and scanned the apartment. Needless to say, it was in pretty rough shape. There were piles of paperwork on every available surface, some stacked several feet high. Some of the piles consisted of just wrinkled balls of paper. The rejects, hairbrained ideas and notes that I no longer liked—i.e. The Shit Pile. There were many Shit Piles, and more on the way. I know it was an issue because I couldn't walk in any given direction without either stepping on or knocking over a leaning tower. Paper castles aside, there was also a bunch of old food sitting out on the kitchen counters, and a literal mountain of clean clothes where my couch used to be. Not exactly fit for company.

Regardless of the mess, I lifted my phone and quickly texted back: *Sure. Come on over anytime.*

Tossing my phone onto the bed, I brought my focus back to the now and ran straight to the bathroom. For some reason, I checked to make sure that there was plenty of toilet paper available and that the toilet had been flushed. As I placed a new roll into the mounted wall holder, I looked up and gasped. Although it only took a second for me to realize, those few seconds were still pretty scary. What my brain had confused for a crazed stranger lurking at my shoulder was actually just my own reflection in the mirror above the sink. It had been a while since I'd really looked at myself. So long, in fact, that I barely recognized the face looking back at me. My eyes were totally bloodshot, hair frizzy and unkempt. As I faced myself in the mirror and attempted to pull my hair up into a messy bun, I heard a soft knocking at the front door.

Great…so much for looking somewhat presentable…

When I approached the front door and glanced through the peephole, there was Kate. Alone, she stood there in a baggy hooded sweatshirt and matching sweatpants. Even through the tiny, warped lens of the peephole, I could tell she had been crying. Her eyes were puffy and red, mascara running like wetted ink. Tissue in one hand, oversized purse in the other, she was very clearly out of sorts. This, I wasn't ready for.

"Oh, hey, Sarah," Kate sighed through a stale smile as I opened the door and faced her. Right away, I could tell she was trying her best to hold back her tears.

Frowning, I glanced up and down the deserted breezeway before asking, "What's wrong? Did something happen? Are you okay?"

Solemnly, Kate closed her eyes and lowered her face before lunging forward to envelope me in a big hug. She didn't know back then that I wasn't a hugger, but she would learn. In time, we would grow to know each other. Usually, during a forced hug, I would anxiously wonder, *How long is this supposed to last for? How tight should I hug back? Is this too tight? Do I put an arm around their neck or their waist? Why can't I do this right?*

But, in that moment with Kate, I had known of the thought. I didn't fight against it at all; I just closed my eyes, let go of all those nervous feelings, and let the hug happen. Soon, I could feel Kate's warm tears soaking my shoulder. Although we weren't close friends yet then, my heart genuinely ached for her. After a few tender moments, Kate pulled away to wipe her face with a balled-up tissue.

"I'm sorry," she sniffled. "Ugh, you probably think I'm crazy now, don't you?"

I laughed. "Ha! Yeah, right. That'd be like the pot calling the kettle black, or whatever that old saying is."

"Yeah, I guess you're right," Kate said, withered smile fading. "This must seem like nothing compared to a day in your shoes. No offense."

"You have no idea. And none taken."

Wiping away the last of her lingering tears, Kate awkwardly reshouldered her purse and asked, "Well…is it okay if I come in? Or would you rather me stay out here in the breezeway."

Graciously, I stepped aside and allowed Kate to enter. Bowing slightly at the waist, I jokingly said, "Welcome to the nut house, madame. Come in and make yourself at home."

As Kate walked past me for the living room, I watched her set down her purse on Laundry Mountain before crossing the room to study my many wall-mounted sticky notes. While studying a section of wall that had the word BIPOLAR spelled out with individual sticky notes, Kate casually turned to me and asked, "Bipolar, huh?"

I shrugged. "Yup. Bipolar."

She then left the wall and approached a pile of papers on the floor that had shoe prints stamped on the first few pages. "Mind if I take a look through this stuff? Looks interesting."

"Sure. Knock yourself out."

I hadn't told anyone about my diagnosis. Not yet. And even if I wanted to tell someone, I didn't have any close friends or family to share with. The only real family I had left was my mom, but we weren't on speaking terms. But for some reason beyond my own understanding, I was okay with Kate knowing. I continued to watch as she gathered up a handful of the papers and headed over to the couch. After a few minutes of leafing through the pages, she looked back up at me and asked, "Did you come up with all this stuff on your own? These five phases of bipolar thing, is this your idea?"

"My God, yes! Absolutely!" I couldn't hide my excitement. Taking a seat at Kate's side, I eagerly plucked the papers from her hands and added, "I've been doing a ton of research on bipolar lately. I figured, if I'm gonna fix this on my own, I have to understand everything about it. After a lot of self-reflection and research, I came up with the five phases. It's like a mental cycle that almost always plays out in the same order or sequence. Each phase has characteristics that consistently repeat themselves. Isn't that interesting?!"

Kate paused for a moment before cautiously saying, "I don't know much about bipolar, but I'm pretty sure there isn't a cure for it. Is there?"

"Well, no, there's no cure, but if I can figure out what triggers each individual phase, then maybe I can find a way to stop the cycle before it takes control."

"Oh, I see," Kate mused. "So…is there anything I could help with?"

I thought hard about this. *Why would she want to help me? We barely know each other. What if I say yes and only end up scaring her away? What if she gets a glimpse of what's in my head and decides to never talk to me again? I don't want that…*

Folding the papers in half, I sighed and slowly sank back into my seat. I felt extremely vulnerable, but also safe somehow. It was a new feeling, one that I never considered to exist before.

As I kept my gaze fixed on the folded papers, Kate turned to me and gently asked, "Do you know why I asked to stop by tonight, Sarah? The truth is, I just caught my boyfriend cheating on me. I got out of work early to surprise him and, boy, I surprised him alright. Walked in on my boyfriend and my best friend, both butt-ass naked on my couch. Now I have nowhere to go. In the course of a single evening, I lost my best friend and the man I thought I was going to spend the rest of my life with. God, I'm such a loser."

Sensing her embarrassment, I met her gaze and said, "Stop. You're not a loser. Your boyfriend definitely is, but you aren't." Just before an awkward silence could break the conversation, I added, "Just curious…how much does he weigh? Your boyfriend, I mean."

Confused, Kate looked away, frowning in thought. "Uh, I don't know. Maybe 195 pounds."

"Okay. And how much do you think your best friend weighs? Rough estimate."

"I'd say…128 pounds."

"Congratulations! You just lost 323 pounds of useless fat in a single night! Plus, a couch. Geeze, someone better call Guinness; that's gotta be a new record."

At this, Kate couldn't help but laugh. "Yeah, I guess that's one way to look at it…"

On a whim, I asked, "Hey, have you ever seen *Lord of the Rings*?"

Kate shook her head. "Don't think so. Isn't it a stupid long movie about elves or something?"

"No…it's actually *three* stupid long movies about elves. And they're all about adventure!"

"I love adventures. Please, show me!"

Emotionally revitalized, I left the couch for the kitchen to grab some snacks. Buried in rubbish, I found a half-eaten bag of chips, an unopened king size Butterfinger, and a fresh two liter of Dr. Pepper. "Off to Mordor!" I cheered while raising the Butterfinger above my head like a chocolate coated Excalibur.

After that night, Kate and I became inseparable. We spent months refining the five phases of bipolar model. As a team. The new model included triggers, phase lengths, moods, and mental severity.

Phase 1: Reflection

This phase is the beginning cycle and usually occurs right after a deep depression takes place. I tend to spend this time recovering and reflecting. Focus pointed inward. I tend to stay in this space for about a month.

Phase 2: Content

This is where I just exist. Just going through the day-to-day motions. My brain is fairly still. I am functioning. I don't have any major mood swings—good or bad. I normally stay in this space for about two months.

Phase 3: Mania

This is usually where I start to get into trouble. I'm overly happy and have a ton of confidence. I feel invincible. I feel like there's no challenge too great. I love mania. I feel free. I don't question anything. The noise in my brain starts to pick up, but it's manageable. Everything is manageable. I don't need as much sleep and hardly eat. The amount of time I spend here varies greatly. Normally, if I notice mania happening, I try to stay aware enough to walk myself back out. Avoid any triggers that might encourage or amplify it.

Phase 4: Paranoia

This is a brief phase and the last opportunity to try and redeem myself before the crash. I question everything. I question if people are judging me behind my back. I talk terribly to myself during this time. The noise in my brain becomes unbearably loud. I can't focus. I can't think. I feel crazy.

<u>Phase 5: The Crash</u>

I'm here for a long time. I often stay here longer than the other phases. This is an extremely dangerous place. I'm so deep in my brain that I've lost all sense of logic and reasoning. I try to push everyone away. I have yet to figure out how to come back from this phase. I pretty much have no choice but to let it run its course. This is the only phase that has hospitalized me.

Understanding my bipolar through this model is what has kept me out of the hospital for so long. Well, until now. I know the model isn't foolproof, but that hardly matters now. My best friend is gone. Forever. So, what now? What's left for me here?

PHASE ONE
CHAPTER 12

The loneliness that I feel while in a deep depression is enough to drive anyone insane. Even while standing in a room packed with people, I couldn't feel more pitifully alone. I can't see or hear any of them; I'm way too deep in my own thoughts. All I can hear are those internal voices speaking on full blast:

You're nothing! Zero! Just another burden. A leech…a human parasite…

No one really loves you! And if they say they do, they're lying! All of 'em are lying right to your face.

Face it, you're unlovable. Always have been, always will be…

If you died, not a single person would care. Not one soul would mourn your passing. Not…one…

One of the worst parts of depression is all the unsolicited advice you get from other people. I can always tell who has and hasn't experienced depression just based on the way they talk about it. Ignorant people will always say dumb things like:

"Don't worry; you'll pull through this. Just gotta try a little harder."

"Oh, stop—you just like being miserable. Cheer up already."

"But you have such a great life. What could you possibly have to be sad about? Get over it already."

The truth is this. I really am trying. Every single day, I am.

I go to great lengths to avoid any triggers that might set me on a path towards deep depression or mania. Honest. But that's all easier said than done; something as small as a compliment or a successful week can throw me headfirst into a manic state. Likewise, something as small as not finishing my To Do List or receiving harsh criticism can send me straight into a crash.

Obviously, I don't want any of this. I mean, who wants to constantly be in competition with themselves? Can you even imagine not being able to trust your own mind—your heart? It really messes a person up. Trust me. This is why I don't like to let anyone get too close. They have no idea what they're signing up for. Bipolar is *my* problem, not theirs. I can't help but think that, maybe, Kate would still be alive had I never involved her in all this.

"Sarah…are you okay?"

Slowly, I open my eyes. There, sitting in a tall chair on the other side of a low table, is Dr. H. I can't pronounce his last name, so, for the sake of brevity, I'm going to keep it nice and simple. I've been forced to counsel with him every single day since being admitted to this psychiatric hospital. Dr. H. is old. He has big, thick glasses that frame his soft, steel blue eyes and bushy, white eyebrows. His hair, mostly white with streaks of faded orange, was probably a fiery shade of red many moons ago. Short and thin in stature, his clean-shaven face holds the same placid expression, no matter the mood or weather. He wears the same exact outfit to every session, too: a plain button-up flannel shirt and faded blue jeans. Although I can't outright place it, there's something comforting about his presence. But maybe it's just the new medication the hospital forces me to take…

"Where were you just now?" Dr. H asks, cool eyes peering at me from over those wide, tilted frames.

Still laying on the long couch, I glance back up at the ceiling and shrug. "I don't know. Lost in thought, I guess."

"What were those thoughts?"

Instantly, I'm annoyed. I'm annoyed that I've been stuck in this hospital for ten days straight. I'm annoyed that this old man keeps asking me the same stupid questions over and over again. He doesn't know me and he never will. This is all just a big waste of time. He knows I'm stuck in a cycle but doesn't care. He's just here to earn a paycheck. To him, I'm nothing more than another meal ticket. Just another screw loose to funnel pills into.

Frustratedly, I sigh. "I'm sorry…but what's the goal here, Doc?"

"The goal is to uncover the real reason why you attempted suicide," Dr. H. answers, his placid tone never changing. "I know this isn't easy for you, but we must work through the deeper traumas of your life in order to find the true source of your problems. It's the only way."

Trauma? My best friend dying, my bipolar—none of this is trauma. These are hard facts of life. Just more pointless bullshit for me to deal with. Nothing can change what's already been done. Not now, not ever. Unless this guy can scrub my brain clean and summon Kate back from the dead, I don't see a point to any of this.

"Like I've already told you," I start to say, biting my tongue, "I did not try to kill myself. It was an accident. As for Kate dying, I'll work through all that on my own terms.

Thank you very much."

"But you must understand that Kate's death isn't the source," Dr. H. continues. "That's only a superficial take. We must go deeper, Sarah. Now, I'd like you to close your eyes, relax, and try to mentally revisit your childhood. Would that be okay with—"

"I'm serious, I didn't try to kill myself. I just wanted some peace and quiet. I know you don't care to hear this, but there was no desperate cry for help. It was just an accident. Sorry to disappoint."

There's a long pause before Dr. H. ruffles his pad of papers and casually asks, "How much, Sarah?"

"How much?" I scoff. "How much what?"

"How much inner silence would be enough?"

Staring at the ceiling, I earnestly consider the question. There doesn't seem to be an answer. I still don't know why I swallowed that entire bottle of pills. I've had many panic attacks before and never once thought about downing an entire bottle of pills. So, what compelled me to do it this time? What changed? I can feel my heart start to race as I look across the table at Dr. H.

"Forever," I finally whisper.

I dab at my eyes before the tears can spring forth. I know I have nothing to cry about. I just need to make a list of the possible triggers that led me up to that moment. I need to study them so this will never happen again. That's the answer. If I ever hope to live a normal life, I must get this right.

"Next question, please," I sniffle, watery eyes now pressed back to the blank ceiling. I have many lists to make and so little time.

Closing his notepad and setting it on the table between us, Dr. H. adjusts his comically large frames and says, "No more questions today. Just a reminder. As you might've heard, tomorrow is family session day. I really think you should try to reach out and invite your mother."

I haven't had a full conversation with my mom in years. She doesn't even know I'm locked up in this hospital. She usually texts me on the holidays and my birthday, but I rarely acknowledge her. I don't understand why she even tries to maintain a relationship with me. I avoid her like the plague. My mom only ever met Kate once. And that was by accident. Unsure, I glance over at Dr. H. and ask, "Okay…can I use my phone to make the call?"

"Of course. Take as much time as you need." Dr. H. then creakily gets up from his chair and shuffles out of the room.

My mom's had the same phone number for the past fifteen years. To this day, I've only been able to memorize two phone numbers—hers and Kate's. I pick up the phone and dial the number from memory. I don't know what to expect from this conversation, but I'm going for it anyway.

"Hello. Margaret speaking."

I struggle to form words, lips stiff and mind instantly wiped blank. I consider just hanging up. Mission aborted. Skin hot, stomach cramping—is this guilt I'm feeling? Hearing her voice for the first time in years is triggering emotions that I never realized I had. I'm sure Dr. H. knows how badly this is fucking with my head.

"Hi, Momma," I say, voice trembling, "It's me…Sarah."

There's a slight pause over the line before I hear her gasp,

"Oh, my goodness, Sarah?! Is this really you?! How are you, dear? Is everything okay?"

"I'm okay," I lie. "Well…kind of. Actually, I'm at an inpatient psychiatric program just outside of Phoenix and—"

"Oh no, what happened?" The fear in her voice sends another sharp pang of guilt through me.

"That's a long story. I called because I have this thing tomorrow, it's called family sessions. It's this dumb thing where the therapists allow family members to join us during one-on-one sessions. Is that something you'd be interested in attending? No big deal if you can't. I understand if you have plans or—"

"Absolutely, I'll be there. What time and place?"

Surprised, I stammer to say, "Oh…uh…it's at the White Mountain Treatment Facility, 11 a.m."

"See you then, Sarah. Love you. Bye-bye."

"Thanks, Mom. Bye."

The call ends before anything else can be said. That very short conversation was more than I'd given her in a very long time. I soon venture out of Dr. H.'s office and down the hallway to my room. Currently, I have the whole room to myself. This will change though. Always does. But I'll enjoy the privacy while I can. Sitting down at the tiny desk in the corner of my room, I fish through the bottom drawer for a notebook. Dr. H. suggested that I start journaling all my thoughts in it, but I've yet to jot down a single word. Spreading those blank pages wide, I grab a pen and start to write:

Dear Journal,

This is stupid. I don't know what to write. I should be figuring out what triggers got me locked up in this shithole. Maybe the triggers aren't outward, but inward. I have no sense of self control. Maybe I never really did. My mother plans on coming here to see me tomorrow. I wonder what Josh is doing. I wonder if he hates me for all that I put him through. I wonder if he told his family about how he had to save my life. I know he'll probably never speak to me again. Kate's dead and I don't know how I'll ever live without her...

I'm not insane; I'm determined.

It's easy to forget that almost every problem we face has a solution. With bipolar, determining the major triggers is a huge part of the solution. I've spent many years learning all the tricky landmines around me. Every day, I avoid them the best I can. Not to brag, but I've gotten pretty good at it. I mean, sure, sometimes I miscalculate a step and end up blowing a foot off, but I'm only human. All humans are intrinsically flawed that way. Especially me. Every detonated landmine sends me straight back to the beginning of the cycle. I try to look at each restart as a new learning opportunity.

If I don't, then this only looks like madness.

A lot of the time, I feel like a hamster on a wheel. Does the hamster realize that it's running nowhere? Just spinning in place—fabricating the illusion of progress. The hamster knows it can get off the wheel at any time, but it always ends up going back. This delusion runs deep. So, if I know all this, why can't I stay away from the wheel?

Maybe I'm looking at this whole scenario wrong. Maybe the hamster learns to enjoy the wheel, regardless of its relevance or meaning. I mean, life is nothing more than a repeating cycle of getting on and off the wheel. If I can learn to just accept bipolar and co-exist with it, will I be happy then? I'm sure it's possible, but I can't even begin to imagine how. Dr. H. has explained to me that perception is everything. To change how we perceive an emotion or action can positively change our reaction. Our very mindset.

Sleepily, I roll over in bed to check my alarm clock. I'm shocked to see that it's already 10:37. I've slept in. Normally, that wouldn't be such a big deal, but today is my family therapy session. My mom will be here in less than thirty minutes. The realization completely sobers me, making my stomach churn with worry. I can still vividly remember the last time my mom and I sat down in the same room and talked. It was roughly five years ago, and I was well on my way to a deep depression.

I close my eyes and search for the memory; I know it's in here somewhere. When I find it, the details fill my eyes like columns of colored sand. In a matter of moments, I'm there again.

After experiencing insane fits of rage, paranoia, and resentment, I decided that I needed someone—anyone—to blame. Somehow, I convinced Kate that I needed to speak to my mom in person. Kate wisely advised me against this, but she also knew I was going to do it with or without her blessing. When we finally took the drive out to my mom's place, Kate placed her hand on my knee and said, "Sarah, I really don't think this is a great idea. Are you sure you want to do this?"

Determined, I looked her dead in the eye and said, "I'm sure. I'm fine if you'd rather stay behind in the car. I got this." I got out of the car and made my way up to the house.

I had a moment of doubt when that inner voice screamed, *No! Turn back! This isn't what you want! This isn't you! Please, don't go through with this!*

On autopilot, I was quick to push the voice away. Bipolar was running the show now. As I climbed the short front steps, I looked up to see my mom standing patiently in the open doorway. I was surprised by her friendly smile, clearly happy to see her daughter coming home.

Well, I was hell bent on ruining that. As she raised her arms out to hug me, blissfully unaware of the absolute carnage of words I was about to unleash, I leaned away and scowled, "No! Don't fucking touch me!"

Even if I lived to be a million years old, I'll never unsee the immense hurt and sadness that came over her face then.

I open my eyes and seperate myself from the painful memory. Rolling onto my back, I feel the warmth of tears as they fall to my pillow.

Maybe I shouldn't run away... Maybe I need to allow myself to feel the emotions that this memory evokes. Observe what happens...

Determined to see this through, I close my eyes and go back into my head—back into the memory.

I delve back in just in time to see myself barge past my mom and into the house. I enter the living room and look around. It looks exactly the same as it did when I was young. Not a single candle or doyly out of place. Various framed photos adorned the four walls of the room, little knick knacks cluttering the dusty fireplace mantel.

I turned to face my mom as she quietly entered the living room, that defeated look still warping her face. I took a moment to just observe her: her light hazel eyes and blonde hair with random streaks of gray throughout. I noticed she was starting to get small creases in the corners of her eyes, deep wrinkles forming across her forehead. Although she had aged significantly since the last time we met, her soft, round face still had an innocent quality to it.

Small hands clasped together, she cautiously approached me and asked, "Sarah, what's going on? What's wrong?"

"You're always nagging me to open up and talk to you, right?!" I barked. "Well, here's your chance! Let's talk!" Overwhelmed with vengeful anger, I stormed over to the couch and plopped myself down.

I knew going into this that I had no intention of listening to anything she had to say. I just needed to blame someone for my problems. Coincidentally, when I was only three years old, my mom was clinically diagnosed with bipolar. At the time, she was twenty-two. One night while studying, I stumbled upon a statistic that claimed fifty percent of children who have a parent with bipolar will eventually inherit the same symptoms.

I held onto this statistic as I watched her slowly walk over to the opposite couch and sit down. Crouching forward, hard elbows digging into the top of my thighs, our eyes met. In that moment, she had to be able to feel the hate radiating from my pores.

"Turns out we finally have something in common," I scoffed. Her new expression told me that she already knew what I was about to say. This only served to fan the flames of my seething anger. "I have bipolar, Margaret." The use of her first name was like a tiny dagger to the heart. It was an attempt to distance myself from her maternal role. Her lack of a reaction further hardened my position.

Small hands now crossed over her chest, my mom tearfully looked me in the eye and said, "Sarah…I'm…I'm so sorry…"

I soon felt the warmth of my own tears. I wasn't crying from sadness, however, but sever irritation. I never had a choice in this. How does she seem so well put together while I can barely make it from day to day? I spent my entire childhood dealing with her emotional instability, and now the instability is all mine. It wasn't until I was much older that she sought treatment for her bipolar but, by then, the damage had already been done. That's why I wanted her to hurt the way that I did.

"Sarah, you're not alone," my mom warmly said. "I understand what you're going through, but please, let me help you. Maybe with some extra help, you can manage this too—"

"Do you seriously think dumping me off on some therapist is going to undo all the harm you've done?!" My blood was boiling; I could barely keep myself seated on the couch.

Patiently, my mom sighed. "I didn't know then what I know now. I can't imagine what that was like for you back then, seeing all my episodes and freakouts. It wasn't right of me. I know I can't take those things back, but I want to support you now. Please, let me help you."

In a very sinister way, I felt like I'd won the battle. The hurt she felt, the desperate pleading—these were an admittance of guilt. Guilt for all the wrong she had done to me in the past. For the first time in a long time, I felt a sense of control. I didn't want or need a relationship with her. Not anymore. For the final nail in the coffin, I'd deny her the one thing she wanted most:

A healthy relationship with her daughter.

I briskly stood up from the couch to scowl down at her. "I don't need you. I have all the support I need waiting out in the car." I then turned and walked back toward the front door. As I headed outside, I saw Kate watching me curiously from the driver's seat. At my back, my mom begged for me to stay and talk, but there was nothing more to discuss. Before her wailing pleas could get to me, I hopped back in the car and slammed the door shut.

Refusing to look up, I grunted, "Please, just go. Drive."

Kate, glancing back over to where my mom wept on the front stoop, softly began to say, "Sarah…this isn't right. You can't just leave her like this—"

"Just go! Now!"

Against her better judgment, Kate put the car in reverse, backed out of the driveway, and headed out onto the road. As we drove away, I tearfully glanced back over my shoulder at the house, but it was already gone. The rest of that car ride was dead silent. I never told Kate what I said to my mom that day. Never told anyone, actually. Either out of shame, embarrassment, or fear that people would call me a monster.

I've hated myself for the way I treated her. My mother dealt with her own mental health disorder during a time when the medical field at large didn't offer much support or understanding. She experienced this disorder while also trying to raise a child and maintain an unhealthy marriage. No one was there for her. I can't imagine the fear and loneliness she must've felt during those times.

I open my eyes again to see it's now 10:55. I roll out of bed, put my hair up in a bun, and walk out into the hall for Dr. H.'s office.

As I'm walking, I hear a familiar voice at my back say, "Sarah?"

I turn around to see my mom. She's standing just an arm's length away, giving me the sudden urge to reach out and hug her. I so badly wanted for her to hold me and say everything's going to be okay. She's changed a little since I last saw her five years ago. Her hair is much grayer now, face softer and lined with a few more wrinkles. But, underneath it all, there's still a beautiful woman there.

Awkwardly, we both just stand there in the empty hallway, staring at each other. I can tell she's unsure whether attempting to hug me will backfire or not. I don't blame her for thinking that either. Fighting back tears, I hold myself together just long enough to say, "Thank you so much for coming. Follow me, I'll take you to Dr. H.'s office." She nods and graciously steps to my side.

When we reach the office, I peek inside to see Dr. H. sitting quietly at his desk. I also notice that the area I normally sit in has been rearranged. The single loveseat has been replaced with two identical chairs, placed side-by-side. Only Dr. H.'s usual high-back chair remains in its original position.

"Good morning, Sarah," Dr. H. says as he looks up from his desk to see us walk in. "And who might this be?" He knows damn well this is my mother, but I play along anyway.

I stand aside as Dr. H. and my mom meet in the middle

of the room to shake hands. "Good morning, my name's Margaret." For some reason, I find it odd that she didn't introduce herself as my mother. I choose to ignore this as well.

Dr. H. cordially bows his head. "Nice to meet you, Margaret. You two go ahead and take a seat over there while I shut the door."

As my mom and I sit down, we both avoid eye contact or conversation. Before joining us, Dr. H. heads back over to his desk to grab his trusty paper pad and fountain pen.

I can already feel my hands starting to get sweaty. I have no idea how this is going to go. Could be okay, or a total disaster. At this point, I don't know what to expect. All I know for sure is that I need my momma. Needing to speak, I raise my hand and say, "Before we get started, I'd like to say something. Is that okay?"

I now have everyone's undivided attention. I feel intensely vulnerable, but also have this overwhelming urge to spill my guts and apologize for everything. I'm not exactly sure this is the right way to go about it, but there's no going back. The time is now. When Dr. H. nods his approval, I turn in my chair and fully face my mom.

"I'm so sorry, Momma. I'm sorry that you ever had to experience having bipolar by yourself. I'm sorry that you had to suffer in silence. I'm sorry that I didn't know then what I know now."

This is a cruel trick that life plays on us all—the inability to appreciate things in the moment. Most of us aren't compassionate about things that we don't already understand. We are so quick to reject those things that we don't comprehend. Luckily, there are ways to redeem ourselves. Having some humility is a good start.

I close my eyes and just sit with these feelings. I'm so exhausted. I've spent so many years trying to see the world around me in simple terms of black and white. Good and bad. But real problems have real solutions. Sometimes, there is no right or wrong way to fix something. It just is. My obsession with bipolar stemmed from my need to see it disappear. All this obsession did was create more problems and heartache for those around me. Kate, my mom, Josh— they're all my victims in one way or another.

I know that this apology to my mom is only just the beginning of our healing journey, but I'm finally ready. I need her and I think she needs me. Between us, we have many years of unresolved traumas to sift through. To mend and heal. Although this is my main goal, there's still another broken relationship left for me to address...

UNFORSEEN CIRCUMSTANCES
CHAPTER 14

I made a crucial discovery that day: being truly honest with myself and others is the key to attaining inner/outer peace. Understanding and accepting that this disorder is something that I'll have for the rest of my life is also integral. My bipolar isn't a problem to be solved, but more of a lost traveler. I'm going to lose my way sometimes, that's a given, but—with the right tools—I can always get myself back on track.

When it came time for me to leave the treatment center, I called my mom for a ride back to my apartment. As the car slides out of traffic and up to the curb outside my apartment complex, I turn to her and weakly smile.

"Thank you, Mom," I say softly, head lowered and fingers fidgeting in my lap.

"No, thank *you*, Sarah," she warmly counters. "Can I call you tomorrow? Would that be okay?"

"Anytime, Mom. Anytime."

After a short hug, I climb out of the car and step out onto the sidewalk. My mom smiles, waving goodbye through the passenger side window before pulling back out onto the road and disappearing around the concrete corner. Content, I turn and head inside.

Upstairs, at my apartment door, I notice that its outer

frame is slightly warped and broken—tiny toothpicks of wood fragments peppering the dark hallway rug. Clearly, the paramedic or cops or whoever had to bust down the door to save me. It takes a little force to open, but I unjam the door with a few hard shoulder bumps. Waiting for me inside is an empty hole of stale darkness. Blindly, I have to feel along the walls for a light switch. When I finally find one, I turn on the lights to find myself standing at the end of the hallway. It's evident that someone had cleaned up during my absence. I take a moment to observe all the neatly stacked papers on my bed. Also, the mountain of mismanaged clothes is now all folded and stacked nicely on the couch.

Somberly, I set my bag on the coffee table and move towards the bed. I take a moment to study the stack of papers. My first thought is to grab the entire pile and throw it in the garbage. Luckily, I decide against that. I must view the five phases of bipolar as a tool, not a cure.

I need to call Josh. I need to know where we stand. I don't know if he still wants to pursue a relationship, and I wouldn't blame him if he didn't. I certainly haven't made this easy for him. Quite the opposite. I pull out my phone and find Josh's name. Soon, my heart is racing to the ringing pulse pressed to my ear.

"Hello?" Josh eventually answers.

Upon hearing his voice, my stomach drops like a brick. I wasn't really expecting him to answer. Hearing his voice brings me both great comfort and sadness. I feel immense guilt for seducing him with my manic charm, only for him to discover the real me—a bottomless hole that feeds on pointless drama and destruction.

Swallowing that neurosis, I clear my throat and say, "Hey…" An awkward silence almost envelops the call as I push myself to add, "I just got home from the treatment center. I was hoping…uhm…I was hoping you might come over so we can talk…"

Nothing. Just the hiss of the open air between us. "Hello? Josh? You still there?"

"Sarah," he suddenly answers, voice impossibly soft, "I'm not really comfortable coming over right now. Sorry…" I can tell this conversation is hard for him, but I feel so vulnerable right now.

What if this is it? I fearfully wonder. *What if he doesn't want to speak to me ever again? But if that's true…why did he answer my call?*

Needing to see him, I try to keep the desperation from my voice as I patiently ask, "Okay, I understand, but I really want to see you. Can we meet at the park instead? Would that be okay?"

Josh silently considers this new proposal. "Well…I guess that would be okay. Meet there in an hour?"

"Sounds good. See you then."

We both hang up without saying goodbye. That formality is dead now. I don't know how to handle all these emotions rushing through me. Sitting on the edge of the bed, I take several deep breaths. In and out, in and out. Slowly, I look back down at the pile of papers at my side. Needing a distraction, I gather the pile and go sit down in the middle of the living room. From there, I sort out the papers into five smaller piles.

Five piles for the five phases.

As I look over my five neatly sorted piles, I feel as if

something is missing. Something important. I grab the first stack and begin sifting through its contents. Suddenly, I realize what's missing from my notes: grief. Problem is, I don't know where it fits into my carefully stenciled plan. But before I can figure it out, the time comes to meet Josh. Leaving the five piles on the living room floor, I gather myself together and leave for the park.

Surprisingly, Josh is there already. I see him sitting—alone—at a shady bench on the far side of the park. I'm grateful that his back is set to me; I couldn't handle the thought of him watching my awkward approach. This feels like the longest walk of my life. My own Green Mile. Beyond the bench is a tiny dog park, and beyond that is a bustling playground full of frolicking children—all of them blissfully unaware of the turmoil in my life. And now, Josh's life, too.

As I approach the bench, Josh turns around, causing me to sheepishly avert my eyes to the ground. I can't make eye contact with him, not now. My heart skips a beat as he stands up from the bench and wraps his arms around me. I love his hugs; they make me feel safe. Like tiny hydrogen bubbles, I feel the stress literally dissolve from my body. Not all of it, but some. I rest my head on his shoulder and remind myself that I need to be more optimistic and trusting. More than anything, I need to not ruin this chance at reconnecting.

As Josh pulls away, my heart sinks. I see his eyes are bloodshot and brimming with tears. At the realization that he's crying, the impulse to turn around and run full-speed back to my apartment is overwhelming. I force myself to face him and acknowledge that I probably play a major role in whatever hurt he's going through. Without a word, we both walk over to the bench and sit down across from each other.

"Hey," Josh says, eyes still sparkling with tears. His smile is different than I remember. The smile I see now isn't genuine; it's a cover. He's hiding something. Something damaging.

Regardless, I return the smile in kind and say, "Hey…"

"How're you doing?" he asks.

I'm already at a loss for words. This man is clearly struggling, and yet he's still putting all the focus on my wellbeing. But I don't want to play this game. I need to know what's going on with him. I need to help him.

"Josh, what's going on? You don't look well."

"I'm fine," he flatly insists. "Really. So, tell me about the treatment center. How was it there?"

I hate how nice he's being despite all the bullshit I put him through. A part of me wants him to get angry and yell at me for pushing him away. I need him to be honest so that I can help fix this. Even though he's falling apart, I can tell he's genuinely worried about me. Something needs to be said.

"Is that really what you want to talk about?" I ask.

I can tell he wants to talk but isn't sure how. He looks down at the bench with an uneasy expression. I decide to just stay quiet. No sense in pushing; Josh will talk when he's ready. Head still tilted forward, I watch as he wipes his eyes, fat bottom lip shivering. My heart breaks. Finally, he looks back up at me. Tears are silently rolling down his rosy cheeks. Fighting back my own set of tears, I hold eye contact. This is the least I can do.

"Sarah…why?" Josh finally asks. In this moment, I come up with a million responses in my head, but none of them are the truth. As my mouth hangs open in quiet suspense, Josh raises his voice and further demands, "Why did you push me out like that?"

Needing to say something—anything—I foolishly blurt out, "It…it wasn't me though; it was my bipolar…" Josh simply shakes his head and looks away. I'm so confused. Even so, I can tell he's more than a little frustrated with me.

"Is it your bipolar? Or are you just defaulting?"

My first reaction is hurt anger. How dare he suggest that I'm using bipolar as an excuse? I mean, the fucking nerve. But when I try to think of a retort that'll really put him in his place, nothing comes to mind. That's when I realize something: Josh didn't suggest that I was using my bipolar as an excuse, my sense of guilt did. Taking the least amount of ownership, I used bipolar as an excuse for my lack of compassion. The least I can do is give him a thoughtful response.

"You're right…I didn't prioritize you," I say in a shaky voice.

Sternly, Josh looks up at me and adds, "Yeah, but I prioritized *you*. Didn't I?" I remain silent. I can tell he just needs to express himself. I'm sure he's been holding onto these feelings for a good while now. "I prioritized you because I love you, Sarah. I've always accepted that you have bipolar. You know that." I watch from across the shady bench as fresh tears start to flow from his beautiful eyes. "I prioritized you because I love you…but you don't love yourself. How come I can learn to coexist with your bipolar, but you refuse to even try?"

Eyes burning, I struggle to find the right words. "Please, Josh, I can fix this," I desperately say. I need him to understand, but now I'm not sure if that's even possible anymore.

Voice softened, shoulders sagging, Josh slowly shakes his head from side to side. "Sarah, the world isn't black and white. Life isn't some long equation that can be solved."

Wow. He really nailed it.

Through a thin veil of tears, Josh continues, "I'm sorry, but I can't be in a relationship with you right now. I just…I just can't."

There it is. The moment of truth. Everything around us—the park, the playground, all the happy people—fades into the static. Everything except for two dogs chasing after a ball in the dog park. For some reason, I'm now hyper focused on them. They're so happy together. As Josh continues to talk to me, I focus on the two dogs, unable to process anything he's saying. All I can do is occasionally nod in agreement, but it's an empty gesture. As I watch the dogs, I realize that we are all living in our own little world. An invisible biosphere of perspective. Even though my world is rapidly crumbling into nothingness, theirs will go on. Unaffected.

"Are you listening to anything I'm saying?" Josh asks, clearly frustrated.

"I'm sorry, but I can't do this," I say as I quickly stand up from the bench.

Josh also gets to his feet but is unsure of what to do. With the bench resting between us like a natural buffer, I turn and smile at him. This smile is to show him that he shouldn't feel any guilt. This smile is also my way of saying goodbye. Surprisingly, Josh smiles back. I'm not sure what his smile says, but that doesn't matter. Nothing can change the state of my reality. Without looking back, I leave the park and return to my apartment.

Alone.

Once there, I put all my focus back on the five piles of paper in the middle of the living room floor. Suddenly, like a bright flash of thought, I realize what's missing. There should be a sixth pile—an unforeseen pile. It would contain all the unforeseen things that randomly show up in all five phases. The unaccountable. After finding a pen and notebook, I label the first page: *The Unforeseen*. I tear off that sheet and lay it face down on the ground. On the next page, I write, *Unforeseen Circumstances.*

Moving down to the first blank line on the page, I add:

1. Grief

ORDER LESS
CHAPTER 15

It's been three days since I met with Josh at the park. In those three days, I haven't left my apartment. Not once. On top of barely eating or going to the bathroom, I've slept maybe eight hours total. If someone were to walk in here right now and see me like this, I'd probably be committed to a psych ward within the hour. For as long as I can remember, my bipolar has always followed a pattern.

However, that pattern has changed.

My tense interaction with Josh has knocked my phases all out of order. I skipped Phase Two and jumped straight into Phase Three. Fortunately, I utilized my mania symptoms and got to work rewriting my bipolar model. I know I can fix this if I can just account for unforeseen circumstances. I've read so many research papers on bipolar 1, bipolar 2, schizophrenia, and borderline personality disorder. I don't understand how there can be thousands of studies done on these disorders but we are still no closer to a cure. I cannot and will not accept this life. If the doctors won't find a cure, then I'll just have to do it myself.

My body is buzzing, thoughts racing so fast that I can hardly focus on any one thing for more than a few seconds. All around me are papers. Papers on the couch, the floor, the kitchen counter, and even covering the bed. I can't help but smile as I look over my many accomplishments. Should have no problem getting back on track. Even though I'm currently manic, I now know what steps to take. I must go back to Phase Two. If I don't, then I'll only be destined for the crash.

Distracted, I look down at the stack of papers in my hand. I read the title out loud: "The Phases Guide to Bipolar with Definitions, Causes, Durations and Solutions." I set the stack down on a nearby table and start organizing them.

Phase 1: Reflection
Phase 2: Content
Phase 3: Manic
Phase 4: Paranoia
Phase 5: The Crash

Suddenly, I hear my phone loudly *ding!* on the far side of the room. I quickly walk over and see that it's a message from Josh.

How's it going? Just wanted to check in.

That's when I noticed the time—2 a.m. If I respond right now, he'll know that I'm manic. Why else would I be up this late? I know Josh read through my bipolar model while I was in the hospital. Feels like I handed him the key to my brain. I'm grateful he would never abuse that knowledge, but it does make it harder for me to hide.

Seeing no other choice, I grab my phone and quickly text back: *I'm okay. Just doing some research.*

Anything I can help with?

In shock, I sit on the floor and wrack my brain for the right response. Sometimes, when I'm manic, I attempt to salvage unsalvageable things. Maybe I need to change my idea of what Josh and I are. But could I handle being just friends with my first true love? It doesn't take me long to decide that I'd rather have Josh around as a friend than not at all.

I would really like that, I respond.

Over the next several hours, Josh and I text each other about my new bipolar theories, Kate, and my mom. It feels nice to be able to express myself without fear of judgement. With Josh, I don't have to filter myself. It doesn't take long before I find myself pretending that his responses are actually coming from Kate. I read his texts with Kate's voice in my head. I know this is a kinda absurd thing to do, but I miss her so much. After a couple hours of lively conversation, Josh stops responding. I assume he fell asleep. Kate would've never passed out mid-texting.

Amateur.

Alone once again, I roll over onto my back and stare up at the ceiling. No one can properly express what grief feels like. It's meant to be experienced, not explained. A part of me wonders if Kate is here with me right now. Where do people like Kate and I go when the big show is over? Kate wasn't religious by any means, but I imagine that she's probably in Heaven. Or some semblance of it.

I close my eyes and imagine what a soul might look like. I imagine Kate's soul—a swirling ball of bright, pastel colors floating around the swaying treetops of a majestic forest. When I try to imagine what my soul might look like, I picture a murky, gray, colored mass. A foggy rock. While Kate had a free soul, mine was bland and petrified. I open my eyes and giggle at the thought, wondering how Kate might react to this less than glowing analogy. She would probably say something like, "Sarah, I love you…but you're a real weirdo sometimes."

Unable to sleep, I climb out of bed and start cleaning up all the papers around my apartment. I open my curtains wide to see the blistering crown of the morning sun. It's been quite a while since I've welcomed its warmth. Grabbing some paper and a pen, I jot down a decent size To Do List for the day. According to the list, I need to take a shower, call my mom, and check in with Dr. H. Honestly, none of these things sound even remotely appealing. So, as soon as I set the list down on my bedside table, it's already abandoned.

Stacking all my pillows up against the headboard, I take the spare candy out from my nightstand drawer and toss them onto the bed. A quick shower, snacks, and binge-watching movies sounds like the perfect day to me.

After I get out of the shower I head to my closet for a shirt. On the way there, I nearly trip over a balled-up shirt on the floor. As I bend down and grab it, my heart instantly sinks. It's one of Kate's old shirts. She used to call it her "Moo-Moo Movie shirt." It's a baggy old shirt with a picture of a cartoon cactus on the front. I have no idea where she even got it from, maybe a flea market or something. I bring the shirt up to my face and immediately pick up her scent. As I inspect the shirt, noticing the faint outline of Cheeto dust on the shoulder, the memories come flooding back.

I miss Kate. I miss her so much that it hurts.

Sliding myself into the oversized shirt, I glance over at the nightstand. Slowly, I walk over and sit on the bed, keeping my eyes locked on the nightstand drawer. For what feels like minutes, I wrestle with whether I should finally read Kate's obituary. Will it help me to work through her absence or only deepen the void she left behind?

Finally, I open the nightstand drawer and grab the folded obituary. I unfold it to see a colored picture of Kate smiling on the front. Although it's not a picture that she would be particularly fond of, she still looks amazing. Vibrant. Opening the flap, I begin to read the obituary. I skim through most of it until I notice my name printed inside.

Kate loved so many, it read, *but none so much as her best friend, Sarah. Sarah brought out the best in Kate, just as Kate brought out the best in Sarah. Sarah and Kate had a friendship that so many will never experience in their life.*

Almost in a trance, I set the paper down on the bed. I think about perception and its meaning—about how I always felt like Kate's parents didn't like me. Their lack of acknowledgement made me feel like I wasn't good for Kate. Or so I told myself.

I don't think I've properly grieved Kate's passing. Hell, I don't think I've properly grieved Josh either. Same goes for my dad. Is there a right or wrong way to grieve a lost relationship? On a subconscious level, I feel as though Kate's just on an extended vacation. Eventually, she will return. And when she does, everything will go back to the way it was. This is an obvious sign that I haven't even begun to accept her death. The thought of her being buried in the cold, hard ground makes my stomach turn inside out. The closest to Kate I can get now is at her gravesite. This thought brings me a small flicker of happiness. I reach over and grab my once abandoned To Do List and add one last item:

Go visit Kate.

ACCEPTANCE
CHAPTER 16

The time has come to reach out. I need a favor and there's only one person left in my life that I trust enough to ask. So, heavy heart guided by my fractured mind, I pick up the phone and make the call.

"Sarah," Josh eventually answers, tone relaxed but deliberate. "What's up? Wow, it's been a while since you've—"

"I need to ask a favor. Not that I'm in any position to ask you for anything, I get that, but I really need you to hear me out and—"

As if hushing a sweet but timid child, Josh softly interrupts, "It's okay, you don't need to explain anything. Honestly…I'm just happy to hear your voice again…"

This simple sentence almost breaks me. I didn't know how badly I needed to hear those words until he said them. Refusing to get caught in the swell of my fluctuating emotions, I numbly shake the tears away and ask, "Would…would you give a ride to the cemetery…to see Kate?"

Without hesitation, Josh replies, "Of course."

I feel like Josh is the only person—other than my mom— that I can openly talk to now. After Kate died, Mags, Sylvia, and Sam all tried to reach out to me. But eventually, their concerned calls and texts slowed, then stopped all together.

That's when I knew the big show was over—draw the curtains and take your bow. Those ties we had are severed. Oh well, what can you do, right? It's not like they were my *real* friends. More like associates. Admittedly, I still think about them from time to time, but I really have no interest in continuing those friendships.

I mean…what would even be the point?

Kate was the glue that held us all together.

Suddenly, I hear Josh's car horn beep from outside my apartment window. He's still uncomfortable coming upstairs to meet me, which is totally understandable. After the shitshow he walked into the last time he was up here, I don't blame him one bit. I glance outside to see a slight downcast of rain, a soft drizzle. As I'm looking at it, measuring its density, the watery mist intensifies. In a matter of moments, the light spatter turns to heavy, strong gusts of wind turning the raindrops on their heads. Preparing myself to get soaked, I grab my bag, leave the apartment, cross the lobby, and sprint for Josh's car. As I fling open the passenger side door, I simultaneously toss the duffle bag into the back seat and quickly sit down. Right away, Josh looks confused. Matching his bewildered expression, I blink raindrops out of my eyes as he slowly reaches over and plucks something from the top of my head. It's a single red leaf. Must've blown into my hair as I ran through the wind and rain for the car.

"Oh…thanks," I mumble, slightly embarrassed.

He nods, dropping the leaf to the center console. "No problem. So, you ready to go?"

Looking away, I nod, then somberly turn forward in my seat—hands stiff and curled.

In truth, I'm not ready at all. Even if I waited a hundred years, I don't think I'd ever be ready for this. But I know it's something I need to do. Extreme discomfort or not, I must make my peace. I must find a way to reconcile the fact that Kate isn't coming back and learn to exist without her. I don't have a real plan yet, but I think visiting Kate's grave is a good start. As we pull away from the apartment, I notice the rain subsides and slowly trickles to a stop.

After a few minutes of riding in absolute silence, Josh looks to me and asks, "If you don't mind me asking…what's in the bag?"

I glance back over my shoulder, studying the bag before answering, "Just some stuff I want to show Kate. That's all."

Dispelling a mild look of curious concern, Josh flicks on his blinker and nods. "So, how've you been feeling lately? Better?"

"I'm fine." Short and sweet. That's how I like it. I refuse to look at him as I speak, keeping my gaze pressed forward to the busy roadway ahead. In the murky lens of my peripherals, I can see him casting curious glances in my direction. I can tell he's worried but doesn't want to press me too hard for answers.

"Huh…" He awkwardly pauses before adding, "Are you managing things okay? Like, day to day stuff." I have no response. I get that he wants to talk about my bipolar, but I'm just not in the mood. Not right now. I have much bigger things pressing on my mind. Almost as an afterthought, Josh clears his throat to add, "I just want you to know that I'm really proud of you for doing this, Sarah."

I hate that Josh isn't Kate, but I also acknowledge that

holding him to the same standard as her isn't fair either. Kate could look at me and know exactly what phase I was in, even if I couldn't. Kate didn't stare at me like I was some sort of twisted science experiment or sideshow freak. I can already feel myself getting irritated with Josh for this—his poking and prodding. My problems aren't a source of entertainment and small talk.

I close my eyes and tell myself to breathe.

Whoa, slow down, an inner voice warns. *You're making a lot of hard assumptions right now. Stop allowing yourself to get all worked up over a bunch of what-ifs and flimsy assumptions. You know in your heart that you can trust Josh; he doesn't view you as entertainment. Remember, just because you have bipolar, doesn't mean you are bipolar. Don't let it beat you.*

After a tortuously long pause, I swallow my hateful feelings and quietly say, "Thanks again for the ride."

In real time, I see immense relief washing over his face. This makes me sad; he was so clearly prepared for me to get mad and blow up at him. Clearly, I'm the abuser in this relationship, and it kills me inside. My past behaviors have conditioned him to react this way. Makes me wonder: is this how I treated Kate? Maybe that is why she was always so generous and caring towards me. I gave her no other choice but to comply with my sickness. Maybe visiting her grave isn't such a good idea. Losing my nerve, I close my eyes again and continue to pace my breath.

As I feel the car come to a gentle stop, I open my eyes to see Josh gently place his hands over mine. Body stiff and shivering, I sit there and focus on my breathing, but it's a real struggle. My gut reaction is to jump out of this car and sprint back toward my apartment. Never look back.

Suddenly, Josh leans toward me and whispers, "You aren't alone in this. I'm right here if you need me."

Like a warm blanket fresh from the dryer, his soothing voice calms my jangled nerves. Slowly, I turn my head and glance out the passenger side window. Whether visited during the night or day, graveyards have such an ominous feeling to them. I imagine what it would be like if every gravestone was equipped with a hidden camera so the dead could watch us walk around their graves. As weird as the thought is, the idea is somehow comforting. Turning around, I pull the duffel bag from the back seat and rest it in my lap. Detached, feeling a million miles away from my physical body, I open the passenger side door and step out of the car.

When I notice Josh get out as well, I turn to him and say, "I really appreciate you being here, but I think I need to do this one on my own."

Solemnly, he nods in understanding. "No problem. I'll be waiting right here whenever you're ready to leave. Take your time."

I can't help but smile, heart melting like an old candle. I still don't know what Josh sees in me, but, in this moment, I'm so glad that he chose to stick around. Hugging the duffel bag tightly to my chest, I turn and enter the open cemetery gates.

There, nestled under a small tree about five rows in, are two headstones side by side. One for Kate and the other for her big brother, Trevor. Standing before the stones, I drop to my knees and read the left headstone's engraving:

Kate Lynn Larsen:
Beloved daughter, sister, and best friend.
May she finally rest in peace.
(1991-2022)

Like moss, I feel as though my legs are rooted to the cold, wet ground. Eyes locked on the simple engraving, my body refuses to move. I just kneel there, squeezing the duffel bag so tight that my muscles start to cramp, and stare at the flat grey stones.

"Hey…" I hear myself say out loud. I don't know if Kate can hear me, but it's the only thing I can think to do. "I see they put you under a tree. That's nice. I know how much you hate the heat." I reflexively pause for a moment, as if waiting for a response. I look up and see the sun begin to peek around the distant bodies of dark rainclouds. Typical Arizona weather. Torrential rain one-minute, sunny blue skies the next. I get a sudden boost of excitement as I look down at the duffel bag and remember its contents.

"Oh, I brought something to show you," I say as I come to sit down before the twin headstones. I ignore the fact that my pants are getting soaked from the dewy grass as I place the duffel bag between us, unzip the top, pull out Kate's old Moo-moo movie shirt, the last letter she ever wrote me, and stack them. My research papers also join the small pile.

As I pull out a box of Whoppers from the bag, I smile at the headstone and say, "Last, but not least, I brought some of your favorite candy. Don't be mad, but I ate half the pack already. Sorry."

For some time, I sit there and silently stare at the two

headstones. Weirdly, it feels natural to talk here. "Josh and I broke up," I say while nodding my head back toward the cemetery gates. "There's so much I want to say right now…but I don't know where to start. Oh, I ended up in the nut house again. Your fault, by the way." After a short giggle, I add, "Cleaned my apartment earlier today. Started talking to my mom again, too. Going okay so far…I think. I stopped going to therapy again though. You know how I am about that stuff."

As I continue to sit and think about what else to say, I glance over at Trevor's headstone. I become lost in the thought of brother and sister finally being reunited. I never got to meet Trevor, but I had seen plenty of pictures. In this moment, there's one picture in particular that comes to my mind. In it, his brown hair is cropped in a neat bowl cut. He's wearing a red polo shirt with ripped blue jeans, hazel eyes sparkling in the flash of the camera. What I remember most from the photo, though, is his smile. It looked so real. So unique. To this day, it pains my heart to know that that same smile was hiding such a deep depression.

I look down at the stack of papers before saying, "Oh, I almost forgot to tell you, the weirdest thing happened to me the other day. I went from a phase 1 calm to a phase 3 mania! I jumped an entire phase. I knew I had to find the missing link, so I rewrote the whole system. This right here is what I got so far."

I start flipping through the papers, occasionally stopping to read aloud. I do this for about five minutes or so. The papers get out of order as I spread them out in front of me. "We never accounted for certain unforeseen circumstances before," I continue to explain, "but I have it all figured out now. I think I found the fix. For real this time."

Shuffling the paper back together and placing them back in the bag, I look down at Kate's oversized shirt. Slowly, I bring it up to my face and take a deep whiff. Draping the shirt over my lap, I look back up at Kate's faceless headstone. With my fingers, I slowly trace the engravings, studying each and every indented letter. I close my eyes and try to accept that no matter how bad I want Kate to talk back, she never will. Not now, not ever. I bring my hands back to my lap and caress the shirt.

As tears start to roll down my cheeks, I gruffly whisper, "It's dumb of me…but I never considered what life would be like without you. I'm so sorry that I didn't come to your funeral. Turns out…you were my unforeseen circumstance. I…I-I miss you, Kate."

I had started to gather my things when a little hummingbird flew over ahead, hovering only three feet away from my face. I pause to watch it float there; its tiny wings blurred with rapid movement. Breathless, I watch as the hummingbird perches itself on the same tree that shades Kate and Trevor's grave. The bird is a beautiful shade of green—fluorescent and bright like an exotic flower. I marvel at how small yet powerfully fast the hummingbird is. As if hearing my thoughts, the tiny bird tilts its pointy head towards me, quietly regards my existence, then takes flight. In the blink of an eye, it's gone.

I close my eyes and allow myself to cry a little bit longer. When there are no more tears left, I kiss the tips of my fingers and press them to the cold surface of Kate's tombstone. I then gather all my things and put them back into the duffel bag. Everything except the letter. Opening the letter and resting it flat against Kate's headstone, I close my eyes and whisper, "I'm so sorry. I didn't deserve you, Kate. You deserved so much better than what I had to offer. It should've been me that died. Not you."

With nothing left to say, I got to my feet and walked away.

As I crossed back through the cemetery and approached the car, I see Josh quickly get out. Always a gentleman, he quickly rounded the car to open the passenger side door for me. The last time he tried this move, I chewed him out real good. Recalling the memory causes me to violently cringe inside, appalled by my own past actions.

"Thank you," I manage to say as I slide into the car and toss the duffle bag into the back seat. I wait until he's back behind the wheel to shyly ask, "Would you want to go grab a milkshake or something? No big deal if not."

Thrown off by the question, Josh studies my face before stammering to say, "Uh…y-yeah. Yeah, a milkshake sounds great."

In seconds, he puts the car into drive and whisks me away from the dewy graveyard. Heart mending, I look back through the cemetery gates and observe Kate's headstone in the growing distance. I don't plan on returning to this place. Not ever. I have to accept that Kate is gone. Nothing will ever bring her back.

PHASE 5
CHAPTER 17

It's been three weeks since I visited Kate's grave. Since then, I feel there's been a profound change in my life.

After Josh dropped me back off at my apartment, I spent hours pacing back and forth. From wall to wall. I searched deep inside myself for one simple thing: a reason to continue existing. I screamed, cried, and even broke things out of sheer frustration with myself. Without even realizing it, I had pulled out chunks of my hair and dug my nails into my scalp. Just then, in between doom rattled sobs, I heard a familiar voice emanate from my bedroom.

"…Sarah…"

Even in my broken state, I knew that phantom voice well. It was Kate's.

Rushing though the darkness, I charged into the bedroom and franticly looked around. But she wasn't there. Nothing was—only the cold, empty solitude of my wrecked apartment. As I weakly turned to leave the room, the voice returned.

"Sarah…you have to stop this…"

If there was any doubt left to the voice's origin, they were quickly dismissed. There was no mistaking those words for anyone but Kate. Shocked, I felt myself begin to shake all over. I wasn't only excited, but mortally scared. But as frightened as I was, I needed to hear more. I needed to talk to Kate.

"Kate?" I asked softly, peering into the layered darkness. Pulse beating in my ears, I stood there and listened to the shadows but heard nothing in response. Suddenly, I felt something hard brush against my left shoulder. I turned quickly to see what it was but was again met with nothing but open darkness.

Coming from somewhere behind the couch now, the voice whispered, "Sarah…you have to stop doing this to yourself…"

This isn't real, my brain insisted. *This can't be real. I must've finally lost it. My mind is broken beyond repair…*

Dropping painfully to my knees, I clamped my hands over my ears and loudly hummed a melody to myself. Anything to drown out the confusing noise swirling all around me.

Now transmitting from directly inside my skull, Kate softly insisted, "Sarah, you need *real* help. None of this is healthy. You must change before it's too late…"

Feeling extremely lightheaded, I lay down on my side let my body curl up into the fetal position. Hands still clamped over my throbbing ears, I lightly rocked back and forth while scanning the room for objects to say aloud.

"TV…desk…couch…bed…carpet…"

Eventually, my mind and body drifted into the stasis of a deep sleep.

When I woke up the next morning, I felt totally normal. I sat up from the floor and looked around, half expecting to see paramedics or the cops. But there was no one there. Groggy and stiff, I crossed the now trashed apartment and opened the curtains to let some much-needed light in. From there, I meticulously inspected every open inch of my apartment, leaving no cupboard or corner unsearched.

Once again, there was nothing. No one. I was and had been totally alone.

Beyond perplexed, I sat down on the couch and began to cry.

Face it, I have bipolar and always will. Who was I kidding with all this self-diagnosis shit? It's not possible to outrun or outsmart a mental disorder, no matter how hard you try. God, I'm such an idiot. My bipolar is just as much a part of me as my skin or bones. We are one entity, one being. I think…I think I know what needs to be done now…

Hands moist with salty tears, I reached over to the side table and grabbed my phone.

"Good morning, Sarah," Dr. H picked up and said after only a few rings. "Nice to hear from you again."

"Hey, Dr. H," I said back, trying to hide the pain from my voice but not entirely succeeding. "Listen, I think I need to schedule an appointment. When is the soonest you could see me?"

There was a brief pause, followed by the sound of ruffling papers, before Dr. H evenly responded, "Looks like I have an opening later this afternoon. Would 1:30 work for you?"

"Sounds good. See you then."

I used to pride myself on being not only brutally self-aware, but totally self-reliant. I never wanted to admit to myself that I needed outside help. I thought, if I studied and theorized enough, I could fix the problem all by myself. But I can't. I need help.

Phone still in hand, I again scrolled through my contacts and called Josh.

"Hey, Josh, if you're not busy, could you give me a ride to Dr. H's office this afternoon?"

Right away, I can feel his concern. "What's wrong? Are you okay? You want me to call someone for you?"

"Nah, I'm fine. Really. I just need to talk to him. That's all."

Josh quietly considered my explanation before responding, "Alright, give me fifteen minutes. I'll be right there."

Later, while riding in Josh's car, I feel his eyes scanning me from the driver's seat. He doesn't come right out and say it, but the strain in his eyes told me he was looking for any obvious self-inflicted wounds. Fortunately, the only visible wounds I had were on my scalp from my freak out the night prior. I was able to cover those with a messy bun though. Problem solved. Well…not really, but you know what I mean.

Josh and I didn't speak much during the ride down to the mental hospital. I was hyper focused on what I felt needed to be done. Preparing myself, I decided to start a private conversation with my bipolar-self. I picture my mental ailment as an alternate version of myself, a woman whose only goal in life is to destroy me from the inside out. Regardless of her intentions, I closed my eyes and addressed her directly.

Hey, I know you don't want to hear this, but if we don't work together then neither of us will exist. When I waited patiently for a response but got nothing in return, I sighed and added, *You don't get to control me any more than I control you.*

Still, no response.

Look, this is my body, my mind, and I can't let you systematically destroy me any longer. Hello?! Do you hear me?! This ends now! Oh, so now you decided to be elusive!

"What's that?" Josh suddenly asked.

With a blank expression, I opened my eyes and glanced over at him. "I-I didn't say anything…did I?"

"I swear you just mumbled something about being elusive. Who're you talking to?"

Embarrassed, I felt my face turn hot and stingy as I answered, "Sorry, must've been thinking out loud …"

When we pulled up to the hospital, I didn't immediately get out of the car. Even then, I knew the version of me going into that hospital would be very different from the version that came out. For what felt like the very last time, I turned to face Josh, admiring how perfect he is in every single way.

I love him. I will always love him. He makes me feel alive and smart. I don't feel like an outcast or a problem when I'm with him. Too bad I can't turn back time and do it all over again…only right this time…

Without thinking, I leaned over the center console and wrapped my arms around him in a big hug. I held him tightly. Taken aback by my impulsive action, he just sat there. Unmoving. Eventually, after a few awkward seconds, he slowly raised his arms and hugged me back. I felt his body relax against mine, accepting my touch. Hearts entangled; this was my final desperate attempt to feel that intimate connection we once shared. With a tearful smile, I ended the hug and turned away to pry open the passenger side door.

Before stepping out, I turned back one last time to say, "Thanks for everything, Josh. I really mean that. You're a great friend. I'm lucky to have someone like you in my life."

Returning the smile in kind, Josh gleefully nodded. "Dido. See you soon."

After closing the door and watching Josh drive away, I headed up the stone staircase for the hospital. With each step I climbed, I could feel the unwanted weight of my bipolar falling off behind me. The anxiety of triggers, the phases, the fear of rejection, the unpredictable mood swings—they all just faded into the background of my mind. And even though medication and therapy might not completely take my problems away, it was the only viable option I had left.

Either that, or certain death.

INSANITY
CHAPTER 18

I spent three whole days at the White Mountain Mental Health Facility. My choice, not theirs. I threw myself at the mercy of Dr. H, fully prepared to start the process of antipsychotic meds and talk therapy. I knew once I started hearing Kate's disembodied voice that I was playing a dangerous game. Previously, I had only ever been medicated while staying at the hospital. After getting released, I'd refuse to refill prescriptions or follow up on treatment. I'd just wing it. I think I only got away with this trapeze act for as long as I did because I had Kate to lean on for support. She was my real medication.

Or so I had thought…

Today is different; today marks the first time I've ever refilled a prescription that wasn't Valium. Also, it's been a whole month and I haven't missed a single day of taking my meds. Kate would be very proud of me.

For the first time in years, I've successfully stuck to a schedule. I take my morning medication promptly at 8 am and meet with my mom on Wednesdays for coffee. On Sundays, I take the time to deep clean my apartment—whether I feel like it or not. I cook dinner for myself at least three days a week, enough for plenty of leftovers on the off days. Oh, and I keep in regular contact with Josh. We check in with each other quite often, send each other funny videos, and gab about the weather. I also walk to the park every night and people watch from the same bench Josh and I broke up at.

Hey, beats just sitting alone at home.

One major change I made after getting home from the hospital was my sleeping schedule. Hearing Kate's voice scared me so badly that I had trouble sleeping in my own bed. I kept expecting to hear her voice every time my head hit the pillow. My tiny studio apartment felt too big for me. I needed something smaller. Cozier. Somewhere comfortable but secure. This is how I ended up turning my bathtub into my new bed. I know, I know; it sounds crazy, but with the right number of pillows and blankets, it's actually quite comfortable. The smaller space helps me keep my thoughts in order. They seemed to just float away in the large spaces of the living room. But not here. Every other day I pull all the bedding so I can shower. When finished, I dry the tub out with a towel and toss it all back in again. Easy peasy.

As I lay here in the bathtub, shrouded in soothing darkness, I can't help but think about a documentary I saw once a few years back. It was about people who suffered from schizophrenia. The documentary showed how these people carried on full conversations with themselves—totally unaware of how they looked to everyone around them. They would hallucinate and give detailed descriptions of what they were seeing or hearing, even though no one else around them could see or hear these things.

This made me wonder, *What if they aren't hallucinations? Just because other people can't see or hear something doesn't mean those experiences aren't real. Who's to say that my version of reality is superior to theirs?*

Sometimes, people with mental health disorders refuse to stay on their medications. They don't like how it changes them. Sure, the medication prevents extreme mood swings and keeps them leveled, but often, they experience an overwhelming side effect of numbness. For me, it feels like I'm just existing. No happiness, sadness, or anything else in-between. No feelings at all. Just being. Like a rock or tree. I know that sounds like a pretty miserable reality to some, but it's one that I'm more than willing to accept given the alternative.

Suddenly, I hear my phone vibrate on the edge of the bathtub. Like an electric beetle, I passively watch it crawl over the ledge and slide into the bowl—now lost in the blankets. Disinterestedly, I fish it back out and open the screen to see a text from Josh.

How's the bath going? he jokingly writes.

I made a promise to myself that I would do everything in my power not to destroy Josh in the same way I destroyed Kate. This means being honest and open—especially about my newfound safe space in the bathroom. I also told him about the new medication I'm on. I think he's relieved to know that my brain is finally getting set to an even keel. To make sure Josh doesn't worry, I made a promise to regularly keep in contact. No matter how I felt.

It's okay, I write back, *2 weeks in the bath has me looking like a prune tho.*

Josh reacts with a laughy face emoji.

I set my phone down and just stare full on into the darkness. I made sure to stuff a towel under the bathroom door, creating an artificial midnight that would never cease. I imagine that this is what my brain must look like. No light or cracks in the smooth dome of darkness. I am obsessed with banishing the light.

This same obsession used to be focused towards fixing my bipolar. I left a path of destruction in my wake. Selfishly, I purposely hurt my family and friends, all in the pursuit of self-discovery. But not anymore.

With phantom fingers, I reach out and grab my journal and pen from the bathroom floor. Dr. H advised me to keep a journal of my thoughts. So, I do. Using the flashlight on my phone, I carefully document my feelings in this moment:

Am I insane? I don't know… maybe…

Oddly, I notice that the word insane is commonly used as both an insult and a compliment. Offensive to some, harmless to others. Over the years, I've heard different takes on the word and its meaning. The definition that I like the most goes something like:

"Insanity is doing the same exact thing over and over and expecting different results."

Perspective is everything though. I don't view insanity as a bad thing. I see a person who is determined. They refuse to call it quits. They see a problem and have set themselves to finding a solution. No matter the personal cost. They aren't bad people for doing this; just blinded by their own obsession.

Others might view this person as a problem, delusional. Cursed with a flawed inability to adapt or pivot. People might think that they would be happier if they realized what they were doing and stop the cycle. Stopping the cycle for me sounds like a person who is just existing. Simply existing is how I view insanity.

I think, for now, I'll just live with this current version of insanity.

Better this than nothing at all…

ABOUT THE AUTHOR

Birdie is a mental health advocate, writer, and speaker. She has written articles for the International Bipolar Foundation and is a speaker for NAMI. You can find her on Instagram @birdies.bipolar.brain for content on Bipolar and other mental health conditions.